DIG

DIG

Robert Paul Moreira

Frayed Edge Press
Philadelphia, PA

Published by Frayed Edge Press in 2022

Frayed Edge Press
PO Box 13465
Philadelphia, PA 19101
http://frayededgepress.com

Cover illustration by

"Centaurs" is forthcoming in *The Canopy Review*.
"License" appeared in *Bluestem*.
"Beneath the Encino" appeared in the anthology *Along the River II*, edited by David Bowles.
"The Lighthouse" appeared in *Aethlon: Journal of Sports Literature*.
"Born in Blood" appeared in *Breakwater Review*.
"Dig" appeared in *Azahares*. Excerpts in Nahuatl and their respective English translations are taken from Miguel León-Portilla's *Fifteen Poets of the Aztec World* (1992) and John Bierhorst's *Cantares Mexicanos* (1985).
"The Runner" and "Proxima b" appeared in *Langdon Review of the Arts in Texas*.
"Kiki" was commissioned by Mary Lily Garza, former Principal of Enrique Camarena Elementary School in La Joya ISD in Mission, Texas.
"Heroes Come Home" was co-written with Josiah Esquivel.

Publishers Cataloging-in-Publication

Names: Moreira, Robert Paul.
Title: DIG / Robert Paul Moreira.
Description: Philadelphia, PA : Frayed Edge Press, 2020.
Identifiers: LCCN 2022937811 | ISBN 9781642510416 (pbk.) | ISBN 9781642510423 (ebook)
Subjects: LCSH: American drama—Hispanic American authors. | Families—Fiction. | Hispanic Americans—Fiction. | Man-woman relationships—Fiction. | Short stories— Hispanic authors.| BISAC: FICTION / Hispanic & Latino. | FICTION / Short Stories. | DRAMA / American / General.
Classification: LCC PS3613.O74 D54 2022 | DDC 813 M67--dc23
LC record available at https://lccn.loc.gov/2022937811

To Boston Mat, for taking that chance.

Contents

vivo
Centaurs   3
Mom Spit Blood   7
License   19

situ
Beneath the Encino   33
The Lighthouse   39
Born in Blood   51

utero
Caligula Pérez   67
United Irrigation District   97
Anagram   99

vitro
Dig   103
The Runner   121
Proxima b   139
Kiki   153

About the Author   187

vivo

CENTAURS

Put down my Bulfinch and take a gander pregame to make sure no one's looking before pincering the diamond red out of the cellophane bag and showing them to Temo.

"What is it?" Temo asks.

"Four-for-four, baby," I say. "Guaranteed."

"Seriously, man—what?"

I ogle the poster on my locker door.

"Wild Horse," I say. And Temo, he laughs.

Then me and Temo, we pop one each.

And we hit the field before anyone else, all Olympian and shit, and we vacuum Coach's ground balls with surefire feet and hands. And we sweet-spot the BP balls, no problem. And I wonder if Temo feels the same thing I do. The fluttering at the center; like I just swallowed Hermes's ankle wings.

"Pinche, pussy."

"Fuck you."

"Prove it, then."

Right in front of L.A.'s finest, Temo slaps a Jackson into the scalper's palm and gets us two right field first-rowers. I celebrate with a high loogie on Sunset. Temo, he flips-off the badge, so we scamper up Stadium Way like a pair of Prometheuses on 'roids, past cliff-gulped tenements and dogs barking through three-headed convulsions and two endless rows of stop-n-go, kaleidoscope fenders. We stop only to pick up one two-buck bag of peanuts ('cause inside Dodger Stadium they're a Lincoln a pop!) from Don Chiro in the bed of his barge of a truck, always chewing on that silver coin. We dash all the way up and into Chávez Ravine to where the stairs end and the asphalt plateaus into a path that's much kinder to our Achilles tendons. We wade into the thick of the white and blue masses churning elbow to elbow in the wide, midday shadow of the Union '76 scoreboard, watching as the young, the old stretch through the turnstiles like strands of blue-bagged Big League Chew caught at the bottom of a blender.

"Where?"

"Here, Temo. I told you already."

"Then where the fuck is he?"

"He said to wait for him."

"FUCK!!!"

Temo sucks his teeth, stomps his feet. Me, I lick cracked lips, run my tongue into the bloodied crevices, when I finally see Push rise. He chariots towards us in sandals through the thick crowd, all Dodgered up, too, all the way to where Temo's slapping his triceps beneath the mammoth banner of our Dodger idol, Yasiel Puig. Push opens up his Dodgers jacket, his grin a cracked acropolis, and me and Temo gobble it all up like pomegranate seeds. We make our way to the right field pavilion after that, slalom and plop into our seats as the music clarions and thumps through the scoreboard speakers. Through my fleecy mist I turn to Temo sitting next to me. Feet up on the rail, peanut bag on his knees, his chest slowly heaving, Temo stares out into the field with the Gorgon's eyes.

"But no one's perfect."

"Puig...is," Temo says.

"He made that catch yesterday, yeah. But, shit—he didn't even get a hit."

"We...did," Temo giggles.

"On Olympus. Who you think Puig'd be, Temo?"

"Olympus?"

"Yeah."

"Wild Horse...man."

"Nah, Temo. Really."

"The most...the most powerfullest one, then."

"Zeus had problems, bro."

"Wild...Horse...man..."

Temo chortles, coughs. He closes his eyes and doesn't say another word. He falls back on his bed, on his cloud, way up high.

It breaks on ESPN before squashing me, and I can't believe it: seventy-game suspension for Puig, and in the middle of a fucking good season.

"The rest of the season, man."

"Fuck that. And fuck him. Just give me some," Temo commands.

"But I told you, I'm out."

"Fuck you are!"

"For reals."

"Bullshit. Where you hiding it? Where is it?"

"I'm out, Temo."

"Fuck off! Not today!" he proclaims, rising like a thunder cloud. "You're never out. Never. Where is it?"

"Temo, calm down--"

And Temo centaurs on top of me, starts pummeling me, hard.

"Motherfucker! *You're* out? *You're* fuckin' out? You're never out! Where is it? WHERE THE FUCK IS IT?"

And I'm a god, trembling in creation.

Mom Spit Blood

When Jónas reached the edge of the bus stop—the stop with the life-sized poster of Amanda Nunes, her back to the bench, head cocked left, one eye leering; the Feather and Bantam-weight belts draped over both shoulders; arms chiseled and beady and with a pair of Modelo beers balanced on thick biceps trekking up and into two tight, champion fists wrapped in UFC sparring gloves—he licked his lips and did his best to ignore the ants crawling up his thirty-five-year-old hands. He stood just outside the stop and set the plastic shopping bags on the sidewalk and began to shake the deep purple from the tips of his fingers. He caught his breath and peered through the late-afternoon glare into the long block of government homes that seemed to funnel hazily into that distant parking lot he'd just come from. He snapped each of his shoulders and remembered his mother, who had been lumbering behind him, but now was nowhere to be found.

Gloves, Jónas! Gloves!

Playful punches into his ribs swung him into his mother in her plus-sized gown and flip flops, her arms spread wide, her head angled. She stuck out her tongue, chuckled haughtily, waited for something from Jónas. *Bah!* she said, and turned around and plopped down on the thin, green bench beside a pretty girl in red scrubs.

Unbelievable! You did that in my day, walked into the Polideportivo wearing those things, in front of that enormous crowd, and let me tell you, the entire arena would burst into laughter, throw beers at you, and...

He bit the inside of his mouth as she went on and on, shadowboxing the hot air a few times, her triceps jiggling. He focused his ears on the traffic instead and let the sprawling locomotion drown her out. He tended to his fingers still, opening and closing his fists to get more of the feeling back; and as the blood coursed and returned to normal levels he couldn't help but look over his mother to ogle that girl's neatly-wrapped bun of blonde hair atop her head; that silver-crested earring that slivered down and coiled around a dot of a red stone on her right side, an attractive side; that high cheekbone made from the silkiest white skin; her long, lean neck; the graceful way her shoulders hung over the vee of her folded elbow, then surged up and into thin fingers packed neatly behind the spine of a Harlequin holding fast to the girl's attention.

He slapped his hands together before realizing what he had done. The girl blazed a smile at him; his blood did a stop-n-go. He prepared to return the gesture when his mother leaned back and into his perfect view, stretching her water-logged legs out wide. By the time she eased forward the girl had turned away and cocooned into a perfectly curled spine, and Jónas was lost to the damsels and rogues in that book of hers.

...and skin, knuckles, elbows, knees, blood! That's what it used to be about. Not gloves. Not gloves! Now it's all about gloves and not getting hurt and protecting your face and the ref stopping the fight just when it's getting good—Bah! Like I always told you, Jónas, but you never listened: You get in the ring, you should know you're gonna bleed!

He didn't answer. The traffic droned on beyond the curb, spurred on it seemed to Jónas by the steady flow of that relentless south Texas air. He swore he caught the sound of the girl in red scrubs turning a page. And as his mother snickered one last time and reached into her purse and pulled out the large bag of pumpkin seeds she'd picked up at *El Globo*, Jónas let out a deep sigh and decided to surrender to that game he used to play as a young boy while stuck at work with his mother on weekends. Having failed the Mixed Martial Arts "experiment"—two entire summers of bruised shins, quads, and ribs; split lips; and more than his share of swollen shiners—his mother finally put a stop to the embarrassment and pulled him out, deciding that an honest day's work would transform her son into the man he needed to be. So bright and early each Saturday morning, instead of worrying about round kicks to his head, or knees to his chin from clumsy double-collar ties, or having to empty out the spit buckets for refusing to jab or defend, Jónas sleepwalked onto the Number 4 bus and took that twenty-minute ride with his mother to Our Lady of Sorrows, where she used her vintage Polaroid 180 to sell five-dollar photographs after baptisms, quinceañeras, and weddings. While the patrons suffered tight-waisted through the services, and while his mother cracked dirty jokes in Spanish with the other photographers (*Here's one my coach in Díaz Ordaz told me: What do you call a man with 99% of his brain missing?*), Jónas sat on the well-worn steps of the church entrance and passed the time counting passenger-side heads through the car windows that drove by (*Castrated!*). For no reason he could think of (*Good one, Eva! Good one!*), he only took mental tabs of those heads erect and alert against the headrests (*Okay, okay, before Padre Mario comes out, cabrónes: How do you make a pool table laugh?*), each of them teeming with thoughts and dreams towards piano or Kung Fu lessons or Little League games at McAllen Sports Complex or family picnics at Anzalduas Park or the jetties at South Padre Island. Wherever they were headed (*How, Eva? Tell us!*), it was anywhere and everywhere unrelated to the boring work Jónas endured Saturday mornings, with no say in the matter at all (*You tickle its balls.*). And even in the present, over twenty years and a childless marriage later (*Last one, then: What's the useless piece of skin on a dick?*), as head after head hastened by that bus stop, and as his mother feasted on seeds and patted her edemic legs (*Foreskin, no?*), Jónas couldn't help but feel that same powerlessness enveloping him on the fringes of that convection oven of a rectangular enclosure, all of it gathering and breathing life into Nunes behind him (*Uh, we don't know, Eva.*), setting those undefeated elbows free, so that nothing but hard bone pummeled into the back of his head, over and over and over (*The man, pendejos. The man.*).

He palmed the back of his sweat-soaked neck and noticed the heads before him had all come to a stop. At the vanguard and closest to him an old Kawasaki waited on the yellow line, sputtering and roaring with each flick of the wrist from its tanned, tattooed driver. Jónas welcomed those infectious fumes; through sunglasses, the driver gazed well beyond a group of pedestrians walking by, his long black beard nestled calmly on his chest. A rush and rumble of engines, that wrist flicked harder, a heavy boot to the gear shift, the beard bristled, and the Kawasaki led the loud charge away.

Jónas picked up the bags and decided to wait for the Number 2 behind his mother. He was toeing a few of the slavered shells over a crack in the concrete, annoyed at his mother for not chewing, then swallowing the seeds whole the way he remembered Lorena used to do, when he spotted someone new slouching behind the girl in red scrubs. The young man was set into a pair of beat-up black Converse and worn jeans ripped at both knees. Despite the heat, he sported a thick black jacket that reached below his shins, and under that a T-shirt of the same color with COME TOGETHER printed across his sunken chest. Above the phrase a slick set of fingers coiled over a guitar neck flowing into its headstock. A pair of headphones connected the young man's ears, and that brown, bald head they belonged to, to an iPhone he thumbed through with his exposed hand.

And boy was he close! That infuriated but fascinated Jónas, both at the same time. So close—he toyed with himself—that

Come Together could peer over that phone of his and confirm for him whether Red Scrubs was a natural blond, all the way down to her roots; if her left side complemented her right; eau de toilette, Carolina Herrera, he recognized the scent; and with just a little more effort and ingenuity: the title of that book of hers. That familiar sweat began building in Jónas' palms. He set the bags down gently. He wiped his hands on his pants and imagined himself slipping into that coat and black Converse, cautious and cunning and calculating, close enough for the skin on his knees to brush her rump lightly, leaning in ever so slowly, slowly, his breath hovering just over her shoulder, his eyes invading that book of hers, and then...

Here, here, Jónas, take it. I forgot to give it to you earlier. Carmela at El Globo gave it to me. Don't you lose it. She says the specialist there helped her with her legs. You'll have to make the appointment for me, so don't you lose it.

His mother punctuated her command with short bursts of compressed air that projected even more bits of spittled shells at his feet. He stared at that business card in her hand—on the front of it, a wide panorama of the medical complex on McColl and Dove, its countless beige-colored buildings jutting into a cloudless blue sky—and couldn't, didn't want to, didn't know how to respond, when all of a sudden it was eight months ago again, Jónas no more than a teetering mess of nerves hunched over the kitchen table on white knuckles, his eyes averted, his dinner untouched, the refrigerator grousing behind him, Lorena slurring through bitter wine and words—*You!*—the crash of glass—*You asshole!*—following him to the bedroom—*You fucking asshole!*—pushing him to the bed and launching on top of him—*Where the fuck do you go?!*—then throwing her off, saying nothing loud, tipping over her Carolina Herrera, denting the fridge before falling out the back door and into the restless night. He had not seen Lorena since. A postcard—dedicated to "The Sickest Fuck in the World"—arrived at his mother's apartment two weeks later, informing him the pupusas were so much better where she was now, that she'd broken the lease and donated everything to the Goodwill, and that *Doctors Without Borders* had welcomed her with open arms.

He sighed, took the card finally. He caught the faint drumbeats from Come Together's headphones, a hip-hop soundtrack for the moment, while his mother beatboxed new shells onto the sidewalk. He turned to Red Scrubs—bent towards the curb now, still immersed in her book, holding a red bookmark to her right temple. A semi growled into gear. It trundled through to beat the red light, leaving nothing in its trail but the smell of worn diesel in a rush of hot air that wisped the bookmark from the girl's grasp, past that bag of seeds on his mother's lap, past Jónas, and down the sidewalk.

As if his mother had decreed it, Jónas immediately set out after that bookmark. It swooped through and outside of the stop, fluttered for an instant, then dove down the path he'd travelled earlier, landing on a patch of dried-out grass, where Jónas was sure he had it. But before he could put his fingers on it the breeze picked up again and set it dancing past a fire hydrant, then the beaten stump of an old oak, until it finally slapped into the base of a chain-link fence. Stuck like that, Jónas reached down and picked it up. He gave his back to the stop and took a few moments to study that thin piece of cardstock—a smooth red all around, warm and unmarked on either side, its corners slightly worn. He closed his eyes, slowly slid the bookmark under his nose, reveled in that deep breath. He'd just unleashed his tongue when he heard the commotion on the other side of the fence.

A chill raked up the length of his spine; he wiped off the bookmark on his chest. He turned to find a patch of dirt where a little girl giggled in a two-piece, straddling a shirtless boy beneath her. Her black hair teasing his face, she pinned the boy's wrists to the ground before an old woman in a worn white T-shirt with the faded outline of a stop sign on it. With both legs amputated just below her knees, she perched on the relic of a rusty refrigerator, dead and beached on its side. *Get off!* the boy demanded, wriggling to get free, blowing the girl's hair from his face. The old woman leaned back on her palms and seemed to delight in the scene in front of her, her feeble chuckles punching holes into the sweltering air, her stumps rising and falling and waving at Jónas as if welcoming him home.

Give up! she shouted in Spanish as the boy's rump and the girl's knees continued to conjure small clouds of dust with each new struggle. Then the woman's brow wrinkled; she did her best to sit up. She coughed painfully next, collapsing the vertices of that octagon into her chest. Over his shoulder, Jónas heard his mother calling out his name.

He turned to the stop—a black box of tough plastics, fiberglass, and steel that brooded distant and silent in the approaching twilight. He pressed the bookmark closer to his chest, watching what seemed like the last sliver of sun clinging to the tops of those far-off buildings beyond the stop, beyond the other side of the boulevard.

A mechanical snap, a burst of light, and on the other side of that fence, Jónas turned to find everyone staring straight at him.

You see! grumbled the boy loud, heaving the girl off him with a strength he had not shown before. He pulled himself up, slapped the dirt from the back of his head, his forearms, all the way down to his Batman underwear. A long scar, already healed over with tougher skin, ran in a staggered line between his shoulders and down to the dirty elastic at the tips of the two bat ears.

With cackles teetering on the precipice of a new coughing fit, the old woman pressed the camera to her right eye again, snapped a new photo. *Moooom!* The boy stormed off, shoving the girl's shoulder, pounding both fists on the refrigerator, each declarative step gathering those dust clouds that trailed after him into a murky mass.

The boy turned a corner and was gone. The woman hocked on the dirt, wiped her chin. The girl pulled on split ends and grinned.

Jónas started for the stop again as fast as he could, the giggles quickly devolving to a loud laughter that rang in his ears the entire way.

When Jónas turned into the stop, the cyclops that was Nunes continued her watch over the inhabitants unblinkingly—Come Together, slumped the way Jónas had left him, his head a shining bulb of perspiration; his mother, picking tiny bits from her teeth; Red Scrubs, no longer curled, no longer reading, the book cover-down beside her. Nodding graciously through his mother's broken English, she reached in for a fistful of pumpkin seeds.

The man! his mother proclaimed. *Eh, the man—Get it?*

And Red Scrubs erupted into a guffaw.

Jónas rolled his eyes and stabbed his hand across his mother's face, offered the girl the bookmark.

Red Scrubs cleared her throat. Without looking up at him she took the bookmark and shoved it nonchalantly between random pages. She cupped all of the seeds into her mouth, and Jónas watched as she chewed and swallowed everything whole.

Pretty, eh Jónas? Blonde this one, but a nurse too. Remind you of anyone you used to know? Talk to her!

She punched him in the leg this time, knuckled a nerve that sent a ping through his quad. As if on cue, the girl pulled her cell phone from one of her pockets, turned away, and arched over her knees once more.

Forgotten like that, Jónas retreated back to the shopping bags behind his mother. *Dios mio* he heard his mother say. He stared down Nunes in his short flight, jealous of her clenched fists. He faced the street finally and gritted his molars and let the dwindling traffic blur by without his consideration. The thin plastic at his feet rustled in the dark for a moment until the streetlamp flickered on high above, bathing the stop in one oblong shadow that, for an instant at least, felt like the safest place in the world to him.

Whoosh! after vroom! and again the traffic faded; a swath of shells, dry now, hissed across the sidewalk before him. He felt the jolt from Come Together's elbow against his left forearm first, and turning he noticed the jacket completely open now. While Come Together continued to balance the iPhone in front of him, he wrapped the other hand tightly around his erect penis, pulling on it back-and-forth-and-back-and-forth-and-back-and-forth, until those knees seemed to buckle for a bit, his rump thrust the pelvis forward, and a series of milky spurts cast themselves onto those perfectly ironed red scrubs.

Come Together let go finally, remained rump-tucked-in-pelvis, and dangled there. Jónas gaped at the tip of that organ—heavy now, swollen and pulsing and driveling after all the exertion—and he was thrust back into the octagon for the battle royale (*The fight you're proudest of, Eva? Come on, before the mass lets out...*), naked and nervous but tight-fisted (*Yeah, who'd you beat?*), the bell ringing and the cameras popping and blinking out of the din of that smoky, omnipresent crowd (*His father's dick, I hope.*), shuffling then ducking then striking then dodging through every slippery body around him (*Coño!*), suffering each hard jab and kick (*Haha!*), then taking that last uppercut to the chin that snapped his head back (*But, Eva—look at him.*) and spun him round (*That's all he does.*), a feast of ferocity for all of the voyeurs (*What the fuck's the matter with your son?*), until he hung limp over the ropes (*I'm working on it.*), breathing hard and dripping blood through a victor's masochistic grin (*So fuck off.*), ready to dive back in for more (*Just back the fuck off.*).

Jónas lifted his eyes. Come Together pressed both of his thumbs to his iPhone, smirked at him in the full light from that small screen. Smacking his lips, Come Together smiled two rows of crooked teeth. Jónas felt the sides of his own mouth begin to twitch.

On second thought, you know what, Jónas, just give me back the card. You'll forget. I know you. You always do. Someone there has to speak Spanish. You can't do one thing right. You always—AAGH!!!

And he marveled when his mother found the strength to stand so quickly. She pulled Red Scrubs up by her elbow to avoid the mess. An explosion of pumpkin seeds; that Harlequin and cell phone in flight, bursting off Come Together's chest. Cornered, the young man stowed the iPhone in a flash, not his member, and with Nunes eyeballing him he loosened his glutes, straightened up, still dangling, blinking wildly at Jónas over two clenched fists.

Get him, Jónas!

The street lamp blinked again; that grand shadow imploded, unfurled.

What are you waiting for?!

Studying her palms, Red Scrubs screamed frantically.

Carajo! Jónas!!!

And Jónas was sure he caught the Number 2 coming in, screeching wildly in the distance, thrusting its massive frame towards the stop and unrelenting, its wide, grimy windshield and mashed front grill his own punch-drunk face after taking a hell of a good beating.

Where in the fuck do you go?!!!

The blood—which had already attempted to pump through and harden every muscle in his being—loosened his fists first and amassed into a percolating heat in his face. *Jónas!* resounded again; his mother pulled hard on his sleeve. He watched as his hand offered her the business card she'd given him earlier—soggy and creased and crumpled now. She slapped it away furiously, shoved him with that strength he always knew she possessed.

Jónas fell hard on his rump; Red Scrubs let one fly again. From the warmth of the sidewalk he beheld his mother, lunging forward now and latching onto Come Together's jacket. Jónas brought his knees up and into his chest, his hands together, and softly shuffled the shells from his palms. Come Together reached back and clocked his mother on the chin with a hard right. He leapt over Jónas, still dangling in one quick arc, until the dark swallowed him whole.

The Number 2 finally heaved in with a long shriek and sigh before opening its doors. A rush of beaten, penitent heads swarmed from the steps at the neck and tail of that gargantuan green whale, one after the other, slack-waisted after the long day's journey home, the light from those cell phones tonguing all of their faces, faces oblivious to the surroundings, feet trampling shells without mercy, figures casting crooked shadows as they scurried off in all directions into the night.

A forced groan this time, the doors closed, the Number 2 muffled away. The last head straggled by, leaving nothing for Jónas but that curved spine once again: kneeling at the feet of his mother this time, those glossy clumps seeped into a deep red now that ran down in one jagged string between her shoulder blades.

He felt the breeze die. On his hands and knees he waded through that small sea of flattened shells. He found the Harlequin and bookmark at the feet of Nunes, the book's title no longer of consequence to him. He raised his eyes slowly. He searched up and down the length of Nunes' spine until he finally found his name carved deep into the glass.

A jab to the back of his head, then another, and another, turned Jónas around. Red Scrubs towered before him, her breathing loud, the entirety of her pulsing with each lungful. She began to cry; her head snapped back up. She ripped the book from his hands, the bookmark from his mouth, and ran away as fast as she could.

Jónas picked himself up. Following all of the tumult, the night seemed settled into a stillness all around him now—like in a postcard, everything fixed into place without mercy. From one end to the other, he surveyed the expanse of that empty boulevard shackled in a long trail of traffic lights and dark, headless windows and a hard stump of a median that went on and on in either direction. He shuddered at the thought that all the cars in the world had already passed him by.

He looked down at his mother finally, seated open-legged on the sidewalk and hunched over. A white van ripped by, on its side a large poster of a winking brunette in a bikini, taking a bite out of THE BEST PUPUSAS IN TOWN! The hard bone hurt like a whisper, then something in Jónas went *crack!* And he heard that guttural gathering at the base of his mother's throat first; a nasally swell of blood, mucous, and saliva that amassed somewhere deep inside and stretched her cheeks back tight into a joker's smile. She fingered into the pool of blood in front of her, flicked off a few shells, picked up both of her incisors, glared up at Jónas, then let it all out.

LICENSE

You get it all at my DMV, man. I call it "my DMV" because I got the keys to the double-doors that open up at seven o'clock on the dot, letting in the flood of sleepy-eyed men and women with kids, most of them here to get or renew their driver's licenses. They stumble in and snake up against the length of the white wall with their own strings of keys or lidded Stripes' coffees or flaky Pop Tarts in their kids' hands, each of them ogling my Texas State Trooper uniform and Beretta and Stetson as they pass me in silence, even though I know they got questions. I never say a word, just hawk them as they come in, and none of them ever asks me a thing. When they come in they slouch against the counters by the wall instead and pretend to read the flyers on the walls with the instructions in English, even though the Spanish ones hang just beneath. I chuckle seeing that. Shit, one look from me and any kid straying from his or her parent against that wall knows I mean business. I brush two fingers over my State Trooper badge above my left-breast pocket right after that, proud, then flick dust off my name tag on the other side, making sure "GARCÍA" is shining bright. I walk over to my spot by Rita's booth and wait for her to get set up and call the first client of the day.

Like me, Rita doesn't let these locals give her any shit. Like me, she likes things to run smooth. She's got the toughest job at my DMV, I think, tougher than me even, in charge of giving all peoples the correct information, both in English and Spanish, on all the forms that need to be filled out, as well as any fees. But what Rita hates most is having to answer the same stupid questions twice, and that happens a lot where we work. She yells at anyone who doesn't understand her when she knows she's right, even sends people to the back of the line if they get to arguing with her too much. She winks at me whenever one more victim makes his or her way to the end of the line and does that thing with her fake-blonde hair where she curls it behind both of her pretty little ears. Mmm.

The first time I fucked Rita was on top of the desk in my back office that one night after everyone had gone home. She grabbed me by my badge and threw off my Stetson and straight out told me that she'd had a hard day and to go and lock the front doors and hurry back. I rushed back and pumped while she puffed, and after two sets of that and the sight of her wobbly thighs, I figured we were all but done.

I pulled up my pants, tucked my shirt back in. Rita stayed naked, though, spread out on my chair, her feet up on my desk, and I liked that she felt comfortable. I liked it so much I reached into the bottom drawer and pulled out a well-rattled pint of bourbon and unscrewed the top. She took the first swig, tossed me the bottle, and began to tell me about what had happened during my lunch break that got her so riled up.

"These people, Johnny. I get so irritated."

"Yeah," I said, the bourbon burning nice and slow.

"I mean, I'm Mexican, too. My parents crossed over from Reynosa and worked in the fields when I was a kid. But I took the time to learn to speak proper English. These people, they switch the English and the Spanish every other word, butcher the language. Drives me crazy."

I stole another swig, nodded with my eyes glued to her thick, dark nipples, then imagined both of her parents as sweaty clumps under the hot south Texas sun, pulling out onions by their long green hairs on someone's orders, Rita sitting in the Plymouth with all the windows rolled down, her feet hanging out, reciting her vowels and consonants. I thought of my own father, too, for some reason, Saturnino García, as my mother referred to him on those rare occasions she even mentioned him, somewhere up north in Illinois or Michigan or Ohio, thinking incessantly about me, working, she'd say, and so anxious to get back home to us.

"That one kid, Johnny," Rita went on, "he just got on my last nerve. I mean, with the sign right in front of him, he asks if he has to stand in line to renew his license. And worse, he asks me flip-flopping the English and the Spanish—Do I have to stand in the *linea* to renew my *licencia?*—like that, sounding as dumb as he looked."

"But that's every day here, Rita," I said, swapping her the bourbon. "It's where we live and work; it's McAllen. Thought you'd gotten used to the Tex-Mex by now."

"I thought so, too."

"So you sent the dumb fuck to the back of the line, right?"

"No."

"No?"

"I answered his question, Johnny."

"But didn't you say he irritated you?"

"He did. Right down to my core." She sat up, curled her hair behind her right ear in a rush. "But I answered him anyways, before I realized what I was doing. And in Tex-Mex, too, of all things."

I half-chuckled, stopped. Rita took her longest swig yet, leaned back with tears cutting a path down the mascara on both her temples, and I wondered if the liquor had gotten the best of her already. I stood there in uniform, in charge of nothing though, my confusion as thick as the smell of our sex still hanging in the air.

Rita slammed the bottle on the desk finally, wiped her eyes and cheeks, slapped her feet back down to the ground, stood up.

"Hey, Rita. Listen. Maybe we should—"

"Get your ass over here, now," she said commandingly.

She grabbed me by my tie this time, pushed me down on my chair, undid my pants, and there we went again. Rita clawed into my corduroy all through it and yanked on my badge so much I thought my shirt would tear. I let her do it anyways.

When she'd had enough she got up off me and dressed and finished the rest of the bottle all by herself. "I feel like some lo mein," she said, tossing the empty bottle in the trash, so we headed for the House of China on Tenth and I paid for two dinner buffets. While I munched on some fried tilapia and shrimp, Rita slurped up her mound of steamed noodles. "I'm so hungry right now, Johnny. I don't know why. So hungry. We going to your place or mine?" I smiled. I told her we'd go wherever she wanted once she was done. She winked at me while twirling her fork into the web of her lo mein, flicking her wrist, spooning it delicately into her mouth.

The front and the around the two oak trees for $200, the tubby Mexican said. For that I'd get the toughest weed fabric around, good quality red mulch, and some Texas lantanas and red-orange and yellow ixoras to make it all look real nice. I happened to mention the sprinkler system that had come with the repo originally, and after crawling over my lawn and messing with all eight of the heads, he said he'd replace the four defective ones for an extra hundred. Everything, he said in Spanish, for three-hundred dollars. *You cannot beat that price, señor. Anyone with a license will charge you double. Not me. Not me, señor. Never. Never.*

The Mexican hunched before me, waiting for my answer with his veiny, yellow eyes stuck on my State Trooper badge, tugging on the oval of sweat between his man tits on his faded grey t-shirt.

I thought about his offer, hard. I looked down at the hard dirt and rocks and dry stumps that currently made up my "sorry excuse for a garden." Those had made up some of Rita's exact words on Friday night right after telling me "Go fuck yourself, you selfish asshole!" just for poking her in the back with my stiff, six-inch license when she didn't want to, right as she peeled the pavement from my driveway, so that the Mexican's Monday morning arrival seemed the luckiest coincidence in the world. What better surprise for Rita than to come back home to bright Texas lantanas and ixoras on top of mulch on top of fabric that crushed weeds? She'd love it. She'd love me. Again. Even if I was an asshole (which I wasn't; just horny). For three-hundred bucks, this Mexican was gonna patch things up for me without even knowing it.

Está bien, I said.

I held out my hand to seal the deal. Still stuck on my uniform, the Mexican straightened up, wiped his right palm on his jeans, and shook my hand.

My name is Carlos Pérez, he said in his Spanish.

And I'm Juan—I mean, Johnny, García. Call me Johnny.

Yonny, I will do a good job for you, just like I did for your neighbor last year. Ask him about me. I did his front garden. See, señor?

He pointed over my mailbox and across the street at a two-story brick home with a wide front garden filled with roses and shrubs and other brilliant plants that I couldn't name. Being new to the neighborhood, I couldn't name my neighbor either.

So, Yonny, I will need a hundred to get started. The rest when I am finished. Is that okay?

I nodded and forked over five twenties from my wallet.

Gracias, Yonny. I will go buy all things now. Come right back to get started. Adios, señor.

He climbed into his beat-up Ford Ranger, waved at me as he drove off. I imagined Rita coming up the walkway in awe later that day, my arms wrapped around her from behind, both of us made up, the lantanas and ixoras bowing out to meet their new masters, the red mulch on the fabric just heavy enough to keep down all those stubborn weeds.

That day, that day everyone suffocated all along that postered wall at my DMV, me included. With the air con down, with Rita still pissed at me, I took up shop closer to the everyday clientele near the trash bin, a good distance from my regular place next to the booth of the woman who would love me again. From where

I stood in sweat (I'd helped put up the cheap fans on all four corners of the office, but they only served to toss around the same hot air), I looked over at Rita every now and then. She ignored me like she'd planned it, pretending to give the next guy or gal her full attention, answering every stupid question like she cared, not sending anyone to the back of the line even, and not caring if any of them pocketed the pens she lent them to fill out their forms. So I let the pens go, too. I took off my Stetson for an instant to wipe the sweat from my brow with my handkerchief. I fit my hat back on as a kid's voice sounded "Wow!" and I knew it was all because he'd gotten a sight of me.

Those kids, man. A sight to see that day, especially since the heat had stolen their eagerness to tussle beneath the counters or run up and down the length of the cordoned area where they usually yanked on the thick rope and rattled the poles on their bases until I stared them down. They sat droopy-eyed and Indian style on the cool tiles at the foot of their mothers and fathers instead, tugging on pant legs and flip-flop straps and asking why my DMV wasn't cold like Walmart or Best Buy. Whenever Rita was ready for the next person and the time came to move up, the kids seemed to roll over where they were, reminding me of that legless Vietnam vet by the train tracks on the corner of Inspiration and Frontage whenever he spotted a dollar bill hanging out of a car window. The kids dragged their asses over the lines of dirt-colored grout and onto the next set of off-white tiles, waiting for the fans to cool them down some.

That day, that day I spotted the two white women just as they came in through my doors. To say they were up there in age would be an understatement. One helped the other by the elbow as they both ambled in in short steps, and their foreheads quickly imploded as they surveyed the long line of sweaty, brown bodies. Their popcorn hairdos trembled as the hot air from the fans wisped by. With the heat, at the end of that line, to me, the two women could be nothing else than the whip cream frothing on top of one of Rita's white chocolate mocha frappuccinos from Starbucks. I looked over at Rita again. At her loose hair falling down over her left temple, wishing I could curl it around the back of her ear for her one more time.

And I swear that's when the plan came to me, honest. I made my way down the line, getting my fair share of stares, shooting my own back, up to the end of the row where the white women clung to each other by the first pole in its base.

"Morning, ladies," I said. "Can I help you?"

"Not unless you can cut this line in half, sonny," the one holding the other's elbow joked. She had a twang in her speech that reminded me of my old academy instructor, spitting out his orders.

"I can't even fix the air in this joint," I said playfully, which set them both into tired chuckles.

"It's seething in here," the elbow supporter commented.

"I'm here to renew my license," said the other one and with the same twang. "I lost the paper. The one to do it in the mail. On the phone, they told my sister Jolene I had to come down here to do it. I have trouble standing for long periods of time because of my *ar-thur-itis*, I told them. But no, they said, no. You got to come down if you want your license. So here I am."

The sisters looked away from me for a moment, and I had to turn to see what had stolen them from my charm. Down the length of the line all eyes were on the sisters, at least until they caught me noticing them noticing us. Then all eyes fell down in an instant to study cell phone screens or renewal applications or their slumping kids on the tiles. All eyes stumbled on anything else but us.

"Maybe I can help you ladies out," I said to the sisters. "Come with me."

I grabbed the free elbow and slowly led the sisters past the front of the line to Rita's counter. I flashed a clear palm at the next woman in line and waited for Rita to finish with a zit-faced teenager wearing Jesus hair, a Danzig t-shirt, tight jeans. The woman who would love me again finally looked up at me, so I took my chance.

"Rita," I said calmly, "this woman has problems with her legs. Can't stand in line for long periods of time. We should help her out."

Rita listened and curled her hair behind her ears as beautifully as ever. She looked over at the tired, brown woman and her two kids at the front of the line, then back at the sisters, then finally set her eyes on me.

"Sonny," broke in Jolene, "you know, we don't want to cause any trouble. Shawna and I can wait in line, that's all right. You're very kind to try and help us, both of you, but that's all right. Help the lady there who's next, sweetie. Really. That's all right. Come on, Shawna. We need to go back to the end of the line."

Jolene began to turn Shawna carefully. My head shrunk slightly in my Stetson, and I could feel the sweat running down the back of my neck. I kept my eyes on Rita. The woman who would love me again didn't buckle from my stare, the sweat building in soft beads on her upper lip, tapping her pen on her desk over and over.

"Wait," Rita finally said. "It's okay, ma'am. You can be next."

Jolene stopped with her sister, turned back around. "But, sweetie, are you sure? We don't want special treatment. Don't want to cause any problems. Will no one mind?"

"No," Rita answered. "No one."

"Well, all right. If you say so. Look, Shawna. These nice young people are going to help us out after all."

"Booth Number One. Alex'll fix you up right over there." Rita pointed out the booth closest to the front of the line. "Make sure to have your old license and social security card available."

"All right, sweetie. And thank you too, sonny. You've both been extremely kind."

The sisters slowly melted past Rita's counter and into the designated booth.

"Rita," I said on impulse, "I'm sorry. Let's bury it, no? This ain't the time or the place, I know it, but I don't like us fighting. Wait. Listen first. I got a surprise for you if you come home tonight. You're gonna love it, I'm sure. What do you say? Will you come home tonight?"

The woman who would love me again half-smiled, shook her head, and for a moment it felt as though she would send *me* to the end of the line.

She said "Next!" and I had to move out of the way as the woman with her two kids approached Rita's counter. I stayed in my regular spot and could hear old Jolene and Shawna chatting it away with Alex as he readied to take the photograph for the new license. I'd done a good deed, I thought, so why was Rita still mad? I was trying to figure that one out when a Tex-Mex cowboy in a wreck of a black western felt walked in with a sideways glance, sucking on his teeth at the sight of the line at my DMV.

Them planes make o's like there's no tomorrow, man. That old bat Sellers from across the street sits in the middle of that soccer field behind my house with a Marlboro between his lips, flicking on his remote control and chuckling to the sky each time one of his model barons—he's got two; a blue one and a red one, the rich fuck—goes into a set of loops that please him. He's usually sprinkling ash like that when I'm getting home from my DMV, surrounded by lines of wide-mouthed neighborhood kids all hanging their arms over the chain link fence and taking in the show. When Rita was here, it's what we did too. We used to stroll out there before opening our front door and she would surprise even me by climbing up and over the fence and casting off her flip-flops and sitting herself comfortable on the cool Saint Augustine grass. "Come on, Johnny," she'd say each time, leaning back and putting one ankle on top of the other. But I'd always picture a Texas State Trooper getting his pants caught on a stray wire and falling over in his Stetson as the whole of the audience brought their eyes down from the sky to watch and laugh. "I'm good, baby," I'd say, just as one of old Sellers' barons flew down low enough for everyone on our side of the fence to hear its engine roar, or pulled up fast into a wide, fantastic set of loops, or just edged the tips of one of the tall, sagging palms along the length of the avenue. Rita would partake in the collective "o-o-o-o-h!" when one of the barons came down on the field with a thud and forced old man Sellers to hobble out of his lawn chair to make sure his plane was all right. We'd leave the kids and the planes with the sunlight falling back off the western rooftops, Rita's arm hooked in mine, the short snaps of her flip-flops losing to our laughter at old man Seller's horrible toupee.

But I don't get out there much no more. I come straight home instead and hang up the belt, badge and Stetson for the night and usually cook me up a can of Bush's baked beans, settle it into my gut with a cool Weiser out on the front porch before getting to work on my garden. And that's what I was doing that evening when the Mexican finally showed up after two weeks and explained he was really sorry and that his wife had been in the hospital and his Ranger had broken down and that he had plans to travel up north to catch up with his kid working construction in Ann Arbor, Michigan.

Your money, Yonny, he said in Spanish, offering me a set of sweaty, rolled-up bills.

Keep it, I told him, surprising even myself, as if I was sure he'd meet my father up there, an old fart by now, still planning to come meet his kid someday.

Keep it, Carlos. Y buena suerte.

Gracias, Yonny, he said, getting teary-eyed.

I waved at him as he drove off.

I wish Rita could see it. Yesterday I pinned the weed fabric down, and today, today I'll take a pencil and pad and make sure of all of my measurements first, just like the Home Depot guy said, and poke holes with my pencil where each of the plants will go. I'll do the ixoras, no, the lantanas first, five in total, all spaced out around the outer edge where the sun splashes best in the mornings. By the time old Sellers limps home with his planes tonight I'll have cut crosses into the fabric, spooned out some dirt, and packed in the young lantanas good. Tomorrow I'll do the orange-bulbed ixoras (seven total) and the red mulch, $2.67 for each ten-pound bag (I bought ten). Including the hundred to Carlos, I spent around two-hundred bucks overall. Not bad. Not bad. Maybe I'll do the backyard next. Fit in some guajillos, torchwoods here and there. I need to. It's a real mess.

situ

BENEATH THE ENCINO

Manny stopped playing. He hadn't thrown out the trash. The grass wasn't cut. He was supposed to be in school. He strummed his guitar again, stared out past the drawn bed sheets his mother used as curtains. Waiting was like watching a plant grow.

The door opened. His mother. She was a stocky, heavyset woman in her sixties, wide and durable like any of her bougainvilleas along the front fence. She held a small, white paper bag. Manny struck a G chord, acted normal.

"What'd the doctor say?" he asked.

"What do you care, Emanuel?" his mother shot back. He could always tell when she was angry and at who. Her perfect Spanish included the full first name of her target in everything she said. "You weren't in your room, Emanuel. Juan had to miss work to take me."

"I was in school," he said.

"*Claro que sí*, Emanuel. I'm sure that's where you were."

Manny felt he'd been pricked by a thorn all of a sudden. On the night before, he'd been on good terms with his mother, so much so that she'd even agreed to cook his favorite of all her Cuban dishes—*picadillo* on white rice and fried plantains. But it was clearer than ever now. Even she doubted him.

He looked down. His Yamaha Dreadnought was a shiny black, had a Rosewood fingerboard and bridge, used to belong to his brother when he played. There were fingerprints and smudges all around the sound hole. The jig is up, he thought, all of it. The getting up early and breakfast at Mickey D's and the two to three hours trying out the Les Pauls and Strats at Guitar Center on Ware Road before coming home for a bite with a textbook to avoid any questions—all of that was over.

"Where's Juan?" he asked.

The glasses on his chubby-nosed mother magnified her tired eyes. "Outside. He wants to talk to you, too." She turned and disappeared into the hallway and Manny heard a door close.

He sighed and decided he'd face Juan like this: *Hey. Listen. Nah, just listen. I like delivering pizzas, all right? I like sitting in my car, driving around. And I like to reach into my pockets and the feel of crisp bills. College is four long years and I'm just not like you, smart. You got it? Good. Now leave me the fuck alone!* That's what he'd tell his brother. Finally. Once and for all. Come what may.

He took a deep breath, laid the guitar on the sofa. He peered out the window again and watched Juan move under the arbor of the encino outside as a few small, green-gray leaves let go of their branches and spun down onto the grass. He realized it in an instant, the truth: Fall was well on its way.

Manny hesitated, watched his brother a while longer. Juan stood beneath the encino, his hair the same sheen of a well-washed black bean. He'd taken charge of things ever since their father's death a year earlier. Without Juan, without his job at the university fixing computers, Manny knew: they'd have lost the house. What bothered him, though, was that he never heard the end of it from his mother with questions like *Why can't you just be like your brother?* or *Emanuel, don't you ever think about your future?* or his favorite question that never made much sense but which she asked anyways: *Don't you like girls?* His mother. No matter the occasion, no matter the company, she would always point out how Juan dropped her off red carpet-style in front of the Walmart entrance before parking her Ford Taurus, or how her son mowed the lawn religiously on Saturday mornings, washed dishes every other night, and fed the dog at seven o'clock on the dot. On top of that, Juan even had a Mexican girlfriend and a college degree in Computer Information Systems. *I dropped you on your head by accident when you were little, Emanuel. Maybe that's it?* Manny never answered, took it all in, ignored it as best he could, hoping it would go away. *And what do you think, Juan? Why is your brother the way he is?* Manny watched the two of them discuss him as if he were an experiment they both had a stake in. *I don't know, Amá. I've got to go feed the dog.* Juan's diplomatic answers made it clear as day for Manny: his brother would always be the perfect son in his mother's eyes, the one she could cling onto like fruit on a tree. *You and that stupid guitar. You never listen to anything I say, Emanuel.* He looked at his guitar and imagined the sound of a soft-strung E minor, the first chord Juan had ever taught him, drifting off into the hum of the ceiling fan above him.

Outside, the sun burned fierce. Wincing through the brightness, Manny couldn't help but notice something different about Juan that day. His brother wore a rumpled brow, for instance, and he hadn't shaved. His shirt hung untucked over an old pair of faded jeans. Juan's entire appearance was as unkempt as the grass he walked on. He chewed on his fingernails, circled the encino, seemed to mumble to himself as a car drove by.

Then Juan stopped. He reached up with both hands and grabbed a thick bough. Manny remembered planting that encino with their father years earlier, laughing and swinging from that same limb with his big brother through the years. It bothered him that he couldn't recall the last time they'd done that. He wished he'd written it down, the date, to have recorded the last time. They'd been the same back then, it seemed to Manny. He wondered if Juan remembered that now, hanging there in his black shirt and pants like one of those avocados their father used to steal from the grand tree in Doña Esperanza's backyard. The ones that always fell with a thump, Manny remembered. Some even broke in half on impact, exposing everything inside.

A warm crunch greeted Manny's bare feet on the grass. The weeds brushed against his calves and knees, made them itch, all the way to where Juan hung.

"Hey," he said.

"Hey," replied Juan, looking down at his own two feet.

Manny wondered if it was all an act. It had to be. Juan would boil over any minute, for sure. He was just biding his time. But Manny didn't feel like waiting any longer.

"I know," he started, his back feeling firm all of a sudden, his feet more grounded than ever before. "The fucking grass is horrible! But I don't give a shit, all right? I'm not perfect like you!"

And Manny felt better than a rolling stone. Better than a slow jam composed of his favorite progression of guitar chords. Something inside him spread like roots, urged him on, transformed his newfound courage from a flimsy green to a thick-stalked, determined brown. His lips weren't quivering anymore, and he liked the way he stood.

"I don't like school, and I forget things, to do things. I deliver pizzas, and that's who I am. Not you, okay? I'll never be like you, or what Amá wants. Never!"

And then he waited, realizing the music of his words had come to an end. But he felt ready nevertheless. Ready for whatever his brother might say.

Juan didn't say a word.

Why wasn't he fuming? Manny couldn't understand it. Where was that strong temper of Juan's, the one he'd inherited from their father? Where was that perfect storm always ready and willing to uproot Manny from anything he decided to do, call it stupid and childish, tell him it was time to grow up?

Nothing.

Blocks away, from the tracks on old Highway 83, a rare train whistled. Juan finally lifted his eyes to Manny, and they looked frightened, like the last two raisins in their mother's rice pudding.

"Something wrong with Amá?" Manny asked.

"No, no. She's fine."

"Then, what?"

Juan bore into the grass with the tip of his foot, over and over like some stubborn plow. As if he wanted to make a hole he planned to crawl into, Manny thought. The grass never gave, though.

Juan stopped finally. He dropped from the branch, spoke as he fell into the shape of his bones.

"Ana's pregnant," he said, and he brushed past Manny and went into the house.

Manny clenched his teeth. He stared at the encino and studied the thick, tire-tracked trunk, followed it from the bottom up, until the sun finally poked through the web of branches in a thousand bright pieces. He remembered when he was eight or nine, when the tree itself was young and thin, when he and Juan fought over who could hold the trunk inside the palm of his hand. Juan always won in the beginning because he was older, his hand bigger. Eventually, Manny could do it, too, until the encino outgrew them both.

The train whistled one last time. Inside the house, Manny could hear his mother clamoring to God and the Virgin of Cobre as Juan tried his best to explain. Manny surveyed the sea of grass all around him. Fuck it, he said. He made his way to the garage. He hoped the lawnmower had enough gas left in it for the entire job.

THE LIGHTHOUSE

That all three swore on the Virgin of Cobre to set out the night prior to the start of the baseball season did not bother Lázaro. Other things did. That they were setting out on a Wednesday, for instance, the day reserved for Oyá, and neither brother took the time to visit the shrine in Regla for their ebós, their offerings; that neither wore blue, Yemayá's color, as he'd instructed them to, for safe passage across the ocean waters; and worst of all, upon posing the question, that the brothers teetered on the brink of the ultimate of all sins: neither brought the statuette of the Virgin of Cobre, the patroness of all Cuban rafters.

"Relax," Bárbaro said, pumping air into twin tire tubes beneath the raft. "Teresita's got la Caridad. She'll be here soon."

Lázaro's tongue went numb. Pedrito, the younger brother, on the opposite end of the raft, dropped the paddles he carried. They'd all agreed: no one was to know they were leaving.

Lázaro felt betrayed. All his years as Santero had assured him of one thing: the gods knew arithmetic well. He panicked. He thought if he raced up the sand, back across the Malecón's snaking seawall, past the prostitutes and pimps and salivating tourists, and if he sweet-talked Yeya out of one more dove and a quart of rum, ripped into the tiny throat, and let the blood flow down the sacred ceiba tree, spurted those tired mists, and prayed, *Oyá, Orisha of the Wind, of Wednesdays, I did not know; One more, please*; then Oyá, She would be appeased.

He turned to go, determined to make things right, but not before Teresita shuffled down the dune. The young mulatta glided wide hips to a stop before Lázaro, a blue muscle shirt, no bra. She owned a long, dried tobacco leaf face, with lips like stitches on new baseballs cheating pitchers chewed on for better grips. She looked far from the lipstick-crazed prostitute Lázaro remembered; the same both brothers bedded on winning nights. She carried nothing else with her but the statuette of the Virgin in her hand.

"Here," said Bárbaro, taking the idol, handing it over to Lázaro. He tossed the pump onto the raft. "Let's go."

And it seemed to Lázaro at that moment that music warbled down from the moonlit palms. There, he heard it, an old Benny Moré guaguancó, the kind Yeya loved dancing to. But the title escaped him, and he hated he couldn't remember.

–You coming or not, Lázaro?

Teresita before him. He watched her stand on her lanky toes, stretch her neck out, as if the swelling blackness that was the vast ocean could be looked over like some backyard wall.

–Now or never! What's it gonna be?

His dream of American baseball. It tugged on him from the inside. The Virgin in his hand he remembered. He loosened his fist, afraid he might snap the figurine in two with such a grasp.

–Lázaro!

He sighed. He stuffed the Virgin in his pocket. He hefted his bag with all he owned onto the raft—his catcher's mitt, a few shirts and shorts, an old Russian compass—and eased between the brothers, and the three pushed the raft into Yemayá's domain.

He dreams this:
He is staggering in for a mug of guarápo after five consecu-
tive 0-for-4 nights. The sugarcane juice is warm and it feeds
his tired limbs. Yeya tries, but she's unable to nudge him into
conversation. He decides on the mud-laden back roads back
home, hoping the change in scenery brings his game back

and fast. He is trudging along with cleats still on because he doesn't care. He is racking his brain for the hole in his swing like the hole in his life. Stormy whispers breathe through the palms. The tocorroro late-night carols. Pulsing croaks from river frogs beneath the lazy, metronome moon. Then, a tap on his shoulder, and he is turning. Caked feet. Thin ankles and knees and a lush 'v' between legs and mamey-sized breasts. A mist in her breath. She is wrapping arms around him, making her body heavy, and into mud she is pulling him, on top of her. Like a throbbing worm with cleats still on he feels, from his uniform wriggling, digging in, loving in mud and muggy grass. He is biting her neck and the necklace around it. Red beads around her wrists and the jostle. And she is moaning, she is chanting, she is urging—¡Así! ¡Eso! On top of her. A thrusting and a rhythm. The moon is blurring, and cool pinpricks on his shoulders, and his rhythm, and Mfff!, and changing, and Mfff!, and faster, and Mfff!, and the sky rolling, and the sea inside him overflowing and breaking, and Mfff! Mfff! And it rains. Days later, on puddled fields, he is unstoppable after five consecutive 6-for-6 nights. "Shangó! Shangó!" Yeya is celebrating, and she is taking her necklace, her bracelets, her love, wrapping them on his, Lázaro's, neck and wrists and recharged heart. She is kissing him, adoring him. She is pulling him, rushing him over to Shangó's, the Warrior's, altar, and showing him the Orisha's dance of praise. And Lázaro is dancing, dancing.

Gagging sounds woke Lázaro. He opened heavy eyes to a throbbing sun with the taste of salt thick on his tongue. He reached for his canteen and swallowed the taste away. He watched Teresita, hunched over in front of him, heaving her insides into the ocean.

"Everything's arranged, I tell you," Bárbaro rapped to his brother, his bald head shimmering like fried boniato, while Pedrito fumbled with Lázaro's compass. "Look: we get to the States, get the asylum from los Americanos, and then Chito's cousin, the lawyer, we call him, and Chito said he'll have us playing in a few weeks. Believe that? Us, in the Majors. You, pitching. Lázaro, catching. Me, first basing. Hitting 'em hard. Hitting 'em outta Yankee Stadium. Hah!" Bárbaro soaked in his dreams for a bit before finally paying attention to Teresita. "Coño," he said, prodding the small of the girl's back with his heel. "And you said your father was a fisherman. You're throwing out more than I've seen you eat since Havana. Hah!"

"Leave her alone," Pedrito said.

And the brothers' eyes met; Teresita spits and hawks the glue.

Tight-browed, they inched closer. As catcher, Lázaro was no stranger to fights between pitchers and batters, but he'd never played on a liquid field. He slid over, tried to cut between the brothers, just as Bárbaro flexed a fist-topped arm to show who was in charge and Pedrito thwarted the blow with a knobby elbow, and the compass escaped his grasp and flew into the scuffled air, and the ocean swallowed it whole.

Smooth-browed now, the brothers dove in. Lázaro watched them dip and swerve and gasp and curse in the blue-green like hooked fish in despair. They clambered back onto the raft after a while, empty-handed, shoulders flaccid, dripping their stares down onto the swollen raft boards.

"And now," Bárbaro said.

"The stars," Pedrito offered.

"The stars," Lázaro agreed.

"The stars," Bárbaro repeated.

And Teresita, still retching. And they plunged into their places and waited for the night.

He remembers this:
Drums. Rattles. Shhhhhhhhhhh. Shells.
Sunday is Shangó's day. Hollow rhythms in a humid shack, and Elegguá, Yemayá, Oggun, Oyá, Shangó, all of Them, the

Pantheon, plunked on Their altars. Shots of rum. Scented candles. Fat, steaming cigars. The Negro babalawo stretching a crescent smile in leafy smoke and whispering to the Ancients. Thick chants from Yeya, from the others—"Bajen los Seres o suben los Seres"—over and over, pleading Them down, drumming their feet, palms held high. The sting from the cock's blood, warm, trickling down his face. The Orishas taking over. All of Them. A force from Heaven, slipping him on like a uniform, and a burning and a bearing up and away, and a soaring. Up and over decrepit, salt-tempered tenements and monuments raised to the Revolución, and over sugarcane, tobacco fields, thronging stadiums with rice-rationed, horse-fed, carnival crowds, and over fleecy-foamed oceans, to a pitching mound of a rocky shore, and to a lighthouse, its light-soul burning, brimming, moving—ALIVE! Then the sky falling, and the wind wisping skin like a lover's razor-tipped tongue, and howling, and the lighthouse extinguishing, and darkness.

Awake. Asking the Negro babalawo what it all means, his eyes rolled over white with red rivers inside, still grinning, as he swallows his brimstone-tipped cigar whole.

–Which one, Lázaro?

–Which one do we follow?

They ogled him, the brothers did, with those same eyes that earlier cursed each other. With eyes that begged for answers now, like pitchers on mounds, prompting Lázaro for perfect pitches. Teresita stared too. She sat in her spot, immovable still, as pale and pathetic as ever, her knees up to her chest. The three of them, like hungry-eyed children in line at a government store back in Havana, silent, waiting for their rations.

But why did *he* have to choose, Lázaro wondered. He couldn't understand it. Why him? Pedrito had been the first to suggest the stars, not him, and he'd agreed on impulse, nothing more. He caught himself thumbing the Virgin in his pocket, over and over, picking at her crown with nervous nails.

–Tell us, Lázaro.

–Yeah. You're the Santero. Ask your Orishas. Show us what they can do.

Lázaro lifted his glance up into that blanket of stars, vast and unending. He felt small in the universe, like a makeshift raft set against the ocean. He couldn't understand it, the trembling inside that started him with the sacred mumbles and jolted him into prayer, the Virgin gripped tight:

Babá Mi Shangó
God of the Sky, of Thunder, of my Soul
Which one must we follow?

"That one." Teresita spoke for the first time, and her voice lapped into Lázaro's ears like the soothing waves around him. He followed the girl's arm, then her forefinger, all the way up to a brilliant diamond blazing down in light. He smiled. The star pulsed thick to the syllables in Shangó's name.

–And how do *you* know?

–Yeah. How?

"She knows," Lázaro rushed to the girl's defense. "She's…a fisherman's daughter, remember?"

Teresita half-smiled. Her crumpled face had smoothed, thought Lázaro, and what once was her sickly pallor now resembled a sacred mist all around her wet-brown skin. Bracing her stomach, cringing with her pain, seated as she was in her niche, she reminded Lázaro of Yemayá gawking at him from Her altar back home, and worthy of all praise.

"That one, then," said Bárbaro, clapping his hands. "No use arguing with a Santero *and* a fisherman's daughter. Hah!" He slid over to Lázaro and broke the spell. "Move over next to Teresita. I'm rowing tonight."

Lázaro crawled over and eased in carefully next to the girl.

"You be careful now, Mami," diddled off Bárbaro. "We've all seen Lázaro on winning nights, and this is one of them. You tell me he tries anything, okay?"

"I don't care about that," Teresita said.

"You don't, eh? Sick bitch. We'll see what you care about when I'm cranking 'em outta Yankee Stadium, the girls lining up for me outside the locker room doors. We'll see."

Lázaro settled in next to Teresita. He shifted with the last of Bárbaro's words, and the Virgin in his pocket poked into his thigh, and it hurt.

And with the game on the line, he, the Batter, checks into the batter's box. The Negro babalawo is huffing behind home plate and a catcher's mask. In deep center, the Lighthouse illuminates all. He is digging in, the Batter, gazing out into the ocean of a field, at the brothers, at Teresita, there: first, second, third; inching restlessly off foamy white bags. Like thick pine tar he is rubbing blood into his bat, staring out at Shangó magnificent on the mound, who is looking to first at Olokun, who yells out to Obatalá at second, who is open-mouthed behind Her glove to let Oyá at short know She'll be covering second on the double play; Yemayá creeps in at third, ready for the throw home in case of the squeeze. And Shangó, a grin like a crescent, stares in for the sign from the Negro babalawo, and He contorts into a celestial wind, and the collective gasp from the stands as He lets the ball go. Swinging from his heels, the Batter is, whacking it good, throwing the bat on the ground, marveling at the ball arcing up-up-up-and-away, all the way to the lighthouse, shattering its beacon of a soul.

He can't run.

–Wake up! Wake up!

That a giddy Bárbaro hadn't existed since news of the slugger's batting crown sounded on all the Havana radio stations was of no consequence to Lázaro; or that he willed crusty eyes open, only to find the burly brother balancing himself at the center of the raft, shuffling into a groggy Pedrito's hair, pointing out into the ocean.

–We're here! We're here!

Other things bothered Lázaro:

> his stiff back;

> that taste in his mouth again;

> Teresita pressing warm into his ribs.

"Where..." The girl rubbed her eyes as Bárbaro typhooned in with the news. "Here, mujer. No more Fidel or rationed rice or meaningless homeruns." He giggled like a schoolboy. "Get ready, Teresita. We're eating American steaks tonight. Get ready for American baseball and American dólares!"

Teresita laughed. Lázaro did too. He couldn't help it. In the midst of other wide grins and malnourished teeth he found he could breathe easier, freer. America! He pictured himself in the future, in Yankee pinstripes, crouched behind that irregular pentagon, swallowing forkballs, knucklers, screwballs, anything thrown his way, and the crowd adoring him. He thought of Cadillacs and day games on the road and, well, the occasional woman, of course, prostrate on his hotel-room bed after rum and more rum, and sex and more sex. But, not yet. He wiped his mind clean. The Orishas would need to come first. He thanked Them in his thoughts. He promised all of Them elaborate altars and prayers, rum and cigars after he got settled in. In the space between, where no one could see, Teresita wove her fingers into his. His heart warmed knowing the Orishas understood.

He picked himself up to get a glimpse of his new home, struggling to see anything through the light morning mist, just as the monument fizzled into view, and he couldn't believe his eyes. He blinked furiously, stumbled forward a bit, let go of Teresita's hand. In the distance like in his dreams, plunked on a rocky mass, the lighthouse loomed before him like the last rotten tooth in the mouth of Freedom.

He hurdled into the water with the brothers, as amazed as they were ecstatic, and sloshed up the shallows, the raft in tow behind them, all the way up to the wide sandy shore. He reached for his bag along with them, started the trek inland, the terrain going from sand to hard coral with undergrowth that crunched beneath their eager steps. The sun pounded a hot rhythm on Lázaro's shoulders but he ignored it, focused on the lighthouse clawing ever higher in front of him. Faster and faster the brothers moved towards it. He felt a clammy hand latch onto his forearm and pull him out of his spell. He turned to find Teresita, keeled over and out of breath, and he felt shame for having forgotten about her. He hollered out to the brothers to stop.

"You don't get seasick on land," Bárbaro said, racing back.

"Go," the girl feebly got out. Her face resembled the color of dry sand, thought Lázaro, her eyes paunchy clams. "Just...tired. Need to...rest."

"Let's go, then" said Bárbaro.

"Leave her here? You crazy? Come on," protested Pedrito, helping Teresita stand straight by her elbows. "You can make it. You see the lighthouse? We're almost there." But the girl vomited her answer, sprinkled Pedrito's feet, and he dropped her in disgust, and Bárbaro laughed. The girl turned her eyes to Lázaro. They reminded the catcher of those championship wads on dugout floors no one ever paid attention to. No one but him. Sacred wads he never stepped on, but others did, again and again and again.

He looked a second, then a third time, just to make sure. The sun died, then rivuled with life again through the massing clouds. A distant swell. Crabs dashed off sideways and sunk into their dark, wet holes.

He glanced far. Nothing but a seaweed silence. No buildings, roads, cars, human beings. Nothing but the lighthouse, its rusted dome where its beacon once shone. He wondered when it last had burned, and how bright. He caught his hand in his pocket again, rasping sand grains with his thumb over the smooth, carved wood.

A soft gale like the breath of anger, and with it sand that stung his face, his eyes, his soul.

Her hand slipped coolly into his.

He asked her about the restless wave rolling beneath her skin.

"Four months," she whispered to him, and, then, "Lázaro, I don't know why. I thought...I picked the star because—"

The sun fainted for good. And thunder. Thunder inside him. Thunder beyond the majestic clouds.

"¡Mierda!"

"It's here," pointed out Pedrito to his brother, crouched at the base of the lighthouse. "That's what it says."

"Impossible!"

"Look, Bárbaro," and Pedrito read from the weathered stone just as Lázaro and Teresita approached them:

ADELMIS NORIEGA

TOO FAR FRIENDS

WELCOME TO CAYO SAL BAHAMAS

"Shit!" Bárbaro thundered with the sky. He reached into his bag, brought out his bat, swung wide and wild, casting stones with his eyes at everyone. "Follow the stars, eh? What was it? Trust her? She learned the fucking stars from her fucking father, right?" and he pushed Teresita to the ground.

"Son of a bitch!" Pedrito shouted. "It's not her fault."

Bárbaro's nostrils flared. "I told you: I say what I want, do what I want to her. See," and he rolled the bat in his hands, "I got the wood. You got nothing."

"You can't hit what I throw," Pedrito said.

"Prove it, then. Right here."

"Fine!"

"Lázaro," Bárbaro said, "get your glove out. This ends here and now."

Those cool pinpricks on Lázaro's shoulders. He leered at the lighthouse. Teresita, pleading him not to listen, but her words falling from their altars. He hawked a thick, salty wad on the hard ground, dug into his bag, brought out his mitt, slid it on, twiddled his fingers inside. He stepped on his wad and crouched down while the thunder cracked in the sky.

Pedrito started his windup, looped his left leg down, and delivered something wicked, right past Bárbaro's roundhouse swing, and the ball popped warm into Lázaro's glove, and the catcher was convinced it was all that mattered. "Good one," Bárbaro said, gearing for the second pitch, rolling his shoulders. His brother slurved a smile through the growing rain, stared in with revolution in his eyes, and he curled like a fetus propped on one leg, and birthed a pitch faster than the one before. The bat chopped into nothing but moist air. Bárbaro barked, cracked his neck to the right, to the left. "Come on," he challenged. And on the third day the third ballet, and Pedrito let the ball fly. Lázaro lost sight of it until—*THWACK!*—Bárbaro put his bat on the ball. Pedrito ducked for dear life, but the ball lasered off to the right instead, striking Teresita in the face, splashing her back like a dying wave.

They rushed to where the girl lay, dead. Lázaro picked up the bloodied ball, wiped it off on his shirt, placed it in Pedrito's glove.

"Foul."

"Foul."

"Foul."

They trotted back to their places. Lázaro went into his crouch again. Caught in that same defiant fold in his shorts, the Virgin poked into his thigh as hard as ever, and she laughed, the ball blazing towards him.

BORN IN BLOOD

Marcos stared at the long, slender neck sparkling in the sinking Casma sun, and he couldn't help but marvel at the animal. Even tied by one leg, his gamecock was as graceful as any he'd ever seen, thrusting his head out with every step as if to announce his authority, dipping down to peck at the ground at anything savory. He reminded Marcos of Ares from his father's days when the fights had been held in secret behind the municipio. The same breed too.

No way my Malayo can lose, Marcos thought. *He's the one. The one that'll fix everything.*

The day that changed it all never left Marcos' mind. The day he let his emotions get the better of him. The stupidest day of his life so far. That day, while Marcos' father toiled on the chacra and helped harvest the yearly batch of ripened paguas for sale at the local market, waiting for his son; that day, Marcos and Selene watched a movie after school instead, in his bedroom, and Selene's hair had smelled, had tasted, had dripped sweet sweat like the juiciest mango. In the end, they'd both giggled at their tired, twitching legs.

But a few weeks later, with Selene at the plaza, her revelation she hadn't suffered her monthly blood loss. Marcos thought hard, and his gamecock became the only answer. He convinced Selene like this: *We're young and can't handle this...And what about our future?...Don't you want to travel and see the Estados Unidos and the world?...I do...I'll fight...I'll win the money and we'll take care of this...Don't cry, pues...An early morning trip to Trujillo on the*

*Tres Estrellas, you and me, and it'll all be over, quick as a blade...
You'll see...You won't feel a thing...Don't cry...I promise...No one
will ever know.*

And Selene agreed, but in tears.

Marcos unscrewed the cap off one of the bottles he used to
store his peanut oil. He poured some of the oil onto one hand,
took hold of Hércules, smothered the cock's coat completely, and
the cock shined like a newly minted Sol. Though the sun was lost
behind the tall houses to the west a single heavenly gleam fell
upon Hércules from somewhere, and his dampened amber and
black-blue tail feathers glinted as the cock seemed to pose for its
owner and trainer, turning to the side so as to stare at Marcos with
one unflinching eye.

Perfect, Marcos said to himself.

He wiped his hands on his pants and screwed the cap back
on the bottle. He took out his pocket knife. From under a wobbly
wooden table, Marcos took hold of a cardboard box and poked
holes on the sides so his animal could breathe. He untied the
slippery Hércules, took hold of him carefully, and placed him in
the box and headed out.

Outside, on the corner, in front of the purple home of the archaeologists, Doña Fanny sold her usual hamburguesas beneath the
hum of a light post while stray dogs sniffed and loitered nearby,
waiting patiently for the first dropped morsel from any of the
hungry customers having their fill. Marcos flagged down the
first moto-taxi he saw and it came to a halt on the curb. Those
mutated motorcycles—handle bars, driver's seat on an engine,
a passenger box welded to the rear and covered, the entire con-
traption propped on three wheels—had been the primary mode
of transportation in Casma ever since Marcos could remember.
They sliced through traffic on a busy day like guinea pigs through
grass. On the moto-taxi before him, on the driver's windshield, as
if to taunt Marcos, was stickered the vehicle's name: El Abortado.

The young driver wore no shoes. "¿Las Poncianas pues?" he asked Marcos and his cardboard box matter-of-factly, flipping the back door open, and the boy sneezed without covering his mouth. "Two Soles."

"Vamos," Marcos said. He loaded Hércules onto the seat in the passenger cab. He climbed in right after, and the seat froze the back of Marcos' thighs through his jeans. He closed the door. Black, everywhere—the steel framing, the plastic lining all around—and the only sight of the street outside came through a grimy, see-through portion of the plastic intended as a window and behind Marcos. He could barely make out Doña Fanny's enterprise anymore or the light post or the famished dogs. Inside that man-made cocoon, light and images and sounds and the world outside warbled through the plastic, through the slits in the sharp corners, like everything that made up a hazy dream. *Like falling in a hole*, Marcos thought. He contemplated walking to Las Poncianas instead, but he knew he wouldn't make it on time. "Vamos," he said again loud, slapping his knees a few times, and the driver sneezed once more and sped off.

They came to the Pan-American Highway three sneezes later. Marcos could tell when the ride smoothed from the constant jolt and tremble of the unpaved city streets to the steady purr of the engine on the leveled asphalt road. He'd learned in school that the Highway began as far north as Alaska in the United States, cut through North America, hugged the western coasts of Central and South America, sliced through his own town of Casma and her sand dunes and mango groves and asparagus fields and archaeological sites; ran down south into Chile and Argentina, and ended at the southernmost tip of the continent known as Tierra del Fuego. A long, winding road, full of memories. Suspended in that rumbling, steel-framed and plastic-covered womb, Marcos' mind gave birth to his own life story. He thought of the old days; the days of the old peleadores like his father when the fights had been more about honor than anything else. Marcos remembered how he'd follow his father in secret and take the shortcut through the old market past the fish and guinea pig vendors and into his usual hiding place to enjoy the fights with the other boys. He remembered learning early by watching and the lists he made in his head:

1. Cut the comb and file down the spurs at a young age.
2. Plenty of hierbabuena twice a day for stamina—IMPORTANT!!!
3. Tie the cock often to strengthen the left leg, the striking leg.
4. Use peanut oil on the day of the fight to make the cock shine.
5. Cuts to the neck and torso (some of them) can be healed on the spot rubbing the wound with resin from the ceiba tree.
6. Most cuts will run deep and kill.

And it wasn't long after that the boys started fights of their own. Marcos bought and trained his first gamecock, Atlas, and he was proud when he saw his bird win twelve fights in a row. "Atlas the Champion," everyone chanted. The reigning champion, that is, until the day Jaime arrived.

Jaime came from Carrizales where his father owned a tire shop just off the Pan-American Highway. He showed up out of nowhere one day with a cock tucked under his arm.

JAIME: Who's the champion here?

MARCOS: I am.

JAIME: (shoving his cock in front of Marcos) Fifty Soles pues.

BOY: (to Marcos) That's Fujimori. Be careful.

MARCOS: (to Jaime) Let's do it.

And the boys all gathered round to form a circle and they protected their legs and groins with makeshift bamboo boards held in front of them.

And the cocks were let loose.

And "Atlas!" the boys cheered before Atlas lost a leg.

And Marcos lost his fifty Soles.

And the Earth held Atlas up until he bled to death.

Then, of course, Selene came to Marcos' mind. Pulling the box with Hércules close while the black pressed around and suffocated him, while the driver sneezed outside again, Marcos went back to the time he first met his girlfriend: Independence Day, July 28, a year ago, at the Casma Plaza, the entire town there, and squibs and sky rockets that hissed and crackled and popped into a potpourri of sparkling sounds and colors off the tall bamboo castle, wrapping the beautiful nutmeg-skinned girl in a saint's nimbus. Marcos remembered those barefoot, feet up, bareback-on-the-tile-floor evenings thereafter when the fragrance of wet feathers saturated his skin after tending to his cocks in his backyard pen, and how Selene never failed to offer up her dreams of that nursing school in Lima and her fascination with traveling to the Great Barrier Reef someday. And there was the undressing of Selene soon after too. That day. The undressing. The assisted molting of Selene's clothes with the same fury he usually reserved to rip the labels off the empty water bottles he used to store his peanut oil. Sliding on Selene's chestnut body. Dancing on, with her. That day. And the taste of her cinnamon breasts. And the cocks that crowed outside the window and watched.

The driver slowed and turned and stopped. Marcos wasted no time and thrust himself out of the moto-taxi, and the cool air welcomed him like a midwife's arms. Delivering himself to the outside world, grabbing Hércules tight, he handed the boy two Soles from his pocket.

The driver sneezed and sped off. Marcos watched El Abortado all the way. He watched that emptied, three-wheeled womb wobble and shrink away down the road until it turned and disappeared on the highway.

And Marcos sighed.

A long line of spectators filed into Las Poncianas when Marcos arrived at the entrance. Giddy fingers sprinkled Soles into a locked wooden box before going in. Marcos knew he wouldn't have to pay, though. Peleadores like him signed up at the entrance and went straight into the vivero and stored their cocks there until their fight came up. But for the Final, for the grand prize, Marcos needed to speak to Fausto, the owner of Las Poncianas. After looking around, Marcos caught him greeting people on their way into the arena.

MARCOS: (to Fausto) The Final. I'm good for it.

FAUSTO: You know the rules, chiquillo. You haven't fought in
        a while.

MARCOS: I want in.

FAUSTO: It's Jaime, you know.

MARCOS: I know.

FAUSTO: It's El Pelado.

MARCOS: I know.

FAUSTO: And to the death.

MARCOS: I know that, too.

FAUSTO: Follow me.

Marcos following Fausto into Las Poncianas. Merengue music, booming. Chairs and tables circling the sunken, central arena beneath bright lights and a large Peruvian flag; and families sitting and sipping Inka Colas, waiting, chewing on home-made chips; and the regulars standing around, everywhere, little groups of them huddled in separate clumps and pouring Pilsen Callao beers into single cups to share, as per the custom in Casma, making bets with each other before the fights even start. Fausto strolling past all of this and waving, relishing the success of his enterprise the entire way, Marcos behind him, all the way to the bamboo bar in the rear where Jaime is sitting and drinking a heavy glass of chicha and waiting for his next challenger. And at his feet, still as death in his cage, El Pelado waiting too.

"El Pelado de Transilvania." The name of Jaime's champion. A full-blooded Jeresano, the breed was known for their featherless necks and their ugly, almost anemic appearance. Their savage fighting in the arena too. Fifteen fights and eight neck wounds later had convinced the Poncianas crowd that animal was invincible. Supernatural, even. "Transilvania" was added. And the crowds loved to watch him make every other cock bleed.

Marcos brought the box with Hércules up to his lips. *Right there,* he whispered to Hércules through one of the breathing holes. *Cut that pesqueso! You can do it, chiquillo. Cut el Pelado's neck and we'll watch him bleed!*

And Hércules shuffled inside the box, so Marcos knew he understood.

Jaime grinned when Fausto mentioned the challenge.

JAIME: (to Marcos) You want to fight, eh?

MARCOS: That's right.

JAIME: (to Fausto) The prize?

FAUSTO: Three-thousand Soles.

The total cost of Selene's procedure, as Marcos had calculated it, would be half of that. His cousin at the Trujillo clinic verified it. The bus fare—thirty Soles. The prize would be more than enough.

JAIME: Done.

MARCOS: Done.

Fausto, nodding. Jaime, gulping down the last of his chicha. The music booming, bouncing off Marcos. All the way to the vivero. The vivero next to the ceiba tree where a drunkard is pissing from his knees.

The vivero was an old adobe shack with a thin bamboo door, guarded by a hunched old Quechua with only one tooth to show. Seeing Marcos headed his way the old man curved his sandy lips and flaunted his pearl. Marcos passed him and entered the vivero. Inside, a pair of cocks crowed, one on top of the other, as if arguing over which one of them should live to announce the dawn. Two rows of wood-framed squares lined both walls all the way in, each with its own miniature bamboo door and a bent nail to secure it. The next peleadores stood inside as well. Don Beto fed Bolivar, his Paisiño.;Vasilio checked on Atahualpa's wound from the previous week. They both nodded as Marcos took Hércules out of the box and placed him in his own square.

VASILIO: (to Marcos) Against who, Marito?
MARCOS: Pelado.
Vasilio and Don Beto stopped what they were doing.
And Hércules crowed above the rest.
OLD QUECHUA: ¡Bashilyo! ¡Betho! ¡Ya shiguen pue!
The old Quechua slammed the bamboo door open and rushed in. He hung a large burlap bag on a thick nail set into the brick wall by the door. Don Beto and Vasilio grabbed their cocks and headed out. The Quechua closed the door behind them. The music outside died, and the thunderous Voice introduced the two fighters to the cheering crowd.

Marcos and Hércules remained alone in the vivero. With the fight raging outside, the trainer studied his fighter—his smooth, cut comb; his thick-feathered pectorals; his sinewy left leg; his long tail feathers that rainbowed up and over. Outside, a collective gasp. Hércules straightened up and stared at Marcos with an unblinking, penetrating look. Like a child studying his father.

Everything depends on you, chiquillo, Marcos said to Hércules. *You can't lose. Don't lose!*

And outside, the crowd broke into a frenzy.

The music started again. Vasilio bashed through the bamboo door seconds later, his forehead drenched, a red-stained bundle of white feathers in front of him.

VASILIO: He crowed three times! I should have known! I should have known pues!

And Atahualpa's head fell to the dirt floor with a light thump. And Vasilio kicked it out of sight. And the old peleador stuffed the rest of his cock into the bag by the door. And he turned to face Marcos before he staggered out of the vivero. And his white shirt, streaked with blood, reminded Marcos of the Peruvian flag.

And Hércules crowed.

<u>OLD QUECHUA</u>: Mauwo! ¡Ya shiguesh pue!

The Quechua replayed his role and opened the mouth that was the bamboo door into the belly that was the arena. Marcos' heart, racing. He twisted the nail and took Hércules out of his square. He drew the sign of the cross on himself, on his cock; and the bloodied feathers of Atahualpa poked through a hole in the burlap bag and brushed cold against Marcos' elbow on his way out the door.

And Hércules crowed.

<u>VOICE</u>: ¡Hércules!

The music, still booming. And the crowd, thronging and clapping and cheering. Marcos shuffled through all of it, Hércules gripped tight by his side, all the way to the edge of the sunken arena. He counted nine concrete steps that sloped down into the bloodied, beaten dirt below. He found Jaime there already, El Pelado beneath his arm. And into that wide, illuminated hole, Marcos descended with Hércules.

<u>VOICE</u>: ¡El Pelado de Transilvania!

And the crowd went crazy. And Marcos and his thumping heart and his pulsing body looked up in awe at the halo of spectators above him. And parents pointed down to show their wide-eyed children who they preferred. And most fingers pointed at Jaime and El Pelado, of course, including the finger belonging to Fausto.

<u>VOICE</u>: Three-thousand Soles!

The navajero was a young chibolo with a piece of string in his mouth and a small wooden box under his arm. He finished with El Pelado and moved to where Marcos stood. With the crowd in their uproar he opened his box and carefully removed a curved, two-inch blade that sparkled in the bright lights from above. Marcos turned Hércules toward his own chest. The boy grabbed the cock's left leg, the striking leg, and secured the blade just above the heel, tying it various times over with the string from his mouth until it was on tight. The chibolo sauntered away. Marcos turned Hércules around slowly. He held onto the bladed leg and moved closer to the center of the ring.

And it was time.

JAIME: (to Marcos over the noisy crowd) Ready to lose pues?

MARCOS: Are you?

JAIME: Not even a minute. You'll see. Just like before, cojudo.

VOICE: Ready the peleadores!

The navajero returned to the ring with a large rectangular piece of wood resembling an oversized cutting board with a hole cut into one end of it. Both sides of the board were sprayed pink with blood from previous fights. The blood of Atahualpa and all those before him.

VOICE: Present!

Jaime and Marcos moved toward the boy and his board. Hércules' brilliant neck feathers rose on end instinctively, and he pecked wildly at El Pelado. The champion did the same, stretching out his combat-seasoned neck so far that his scars were barely visible.

There, Marcos spoke to Hércules in his head. He was sure his cock could hear him. *Cut that neck, chiquillo! Cut that neck and make him bleed!*

And the boy balanced the board on the ground.

And Marcos and Jaime crouched down.

And the crowd went silent.

And the boy looked up into the heavens that were the heavy lights.

And everyone waited for the Voice to start it all.

VOICE: ¡A pelear!

And the crowd roared.

And the boy pulled the board away and rushed back and out of the way.

And the cocks were let loose and the dance began.

El Baile de la Muerte. The Dance of Death. Hércules and El Pelado, catapulting themselves off the dirt floor, snapping wings against proud chests, against each other, dropping their bladed heels like hammers onto each other. Hércules, shining and ruffling and bobbing out and into harm's way. El Pelado, squirming and stretching and stomping the dirt floor into dust clouds quickly destroyed by his outstretched, battering wings. Then, with a swift kick and pull, Hércules cutting into El Pelado, ripping into one of his old neck wounds; and Jaime, cursing as the crowd is gasping.

<u>VOICE</u>: Stop!

The navajero rushed in with his pink-white board and thrust it between the enraged cocks and separated them. Marcos and Jaime grabbed their fighters from behind carefully.

That's the way, Marcos congratulated Hércules as he moved back to regroup, and he ran his hand from the back of Hércules' head all the way down his sweaty, peanut-oiled back. He brought his hand up to his nose and took a deep breath. *If success has a smell,* Marcos thought, *this is it. That's an old cortada,* he egged Hércules on. *Get him there again, chiquillo! You can do it! You can do it!*

Across from him, beneath the din of the crowd, Marcos watched Jaime assure the boy El Pelado could continue. The crowd roared louder. The boy and his board, and the fighters and their cocks took the same positions as before.

And the Voice deafened every other noise around as the Dance began all over again.

Hércules, looking great, in a champion stance, dipping his arrow-tip head, backing up, waiting, waiting for the perfect time to strike. El Pelado, cautious, hurting, six toes and two heels firmly splayed out on the ground, kicking up dirt, with a pedator's stare, ready to spring. Marcos and Jaime, across from each other, fists and teeth clenched, mimicking Hércules' and El Pelado's moves, and hoping, hoping, hoping their cock comes out on top.

That's my chiquillo, Marcos shouted. *Take your time! Quick as a blade! You can do it! You can do it!*

Then a combined thrust. And wings in a ferocious flutter, snapping like whips. And Hércules and his kaleidoscope feathers and El Pelado's black ones suspended in the air in one compressed mass. Kicks and cuts in split-second space going nowhere but down.

And a prolonged "Whoooaaa!" from the awestruck crowd.

And Jaime's fist in the air.

And Marcos' heart sliced.

Hércules fell to the dirt with a thump that only Marcos heard. His rooster lifted his head as best he could, flapped his wings feebly. Marcos swallowed. As El Pelado circled away, Marcos saw the thick blood trailing from his blade.

Get up, chiquillo! Get up!

Jaime, yelling. The crowd, with rumbling feet and insatiable hollers, urging el Pelado to give them all what they came to see.

Hércules, still. Marcos felt an overwhelming desire to rush to where his cock lay, to break the rules of the match, to forget about the fight and the money and Selene and the procedure in Trujillo, to save the very animal he'd nurtured and trained and come to love, and to bear him off to safety. He imagined stealing Hércules from the ring and out of Las Poncianas and off onto the Pan-American Highway, running parallel to the sand dunes raked in the light of day by the grandest of all roosters, by God, whose invisible claws were said to be set into the wind that brushed the sand over into even rows. *Running, running for dear life.* He imagined reaching Selene breathless, Hércules barely alive but breathing, Selene's sweet mango hair welcoming them home, and his sore-backed father helping heal Hércules to fight another day. *Everything, everything all right.* But the pungent peanut oil brought Marcos back. He brought his hand up close again. And the success he'd smelled and been so sure of earlier rolled into a taste in his mouth like stale, coppery blood.

Get up, chiquillo! Forget about winning! Just live!

And El Pelado finally turned and found Hércules again. And he charged. And his sable wings bore him high up off the ground like a dark, menacing shadow. And he lifted his heel—his left, his striking, his bladed heel—and the blade pulsed like a dying star.

And the crowd gasped.

And the weight of El Pelado sunk Hércules deep into the ground.

And "¡Vaya pues!" yelled Jaime, both fists in the air.

And "It's over!" the Voice sounded.

And it was.

Selene didn't believe him. Close to ten o'clock, her mother would soon be home, and Marcos knew that. But he sounded desperate and insisted it was important. She put on her favorite jeans, the ones getting tighter by the day, and her chompa to guard against the late-May chill. She headed into the night.

Casma, the city of zigzagging moto-taxis and peddlers and tethered goats on the curb by the butcher store, looked postcard serene beneath a grinning moon. Selene shuffled past the Chifa Hong Kong where fake gold doors closed shut and Marcos loved to eat the tallarín with fried rice. She rushed quickly by the entrance to the slumbering market, its large shadowy archway decorated with a frieze of an ancient Sechin warrior, the pride of Casma's past and the archaeologists with the purple home, a gamecock sketched wildly beneath his arm. Marcos always claimed to know the chibolo who vandalized the archway—a peleador like him, of course—but Selene had never met him. It didn't matter. She trusted her boyfriend now more than ever. She had to. He was right. They *did* have plans. With their future on the line, they were doing the right thing. *What good are we to a child when we don't even have lives of our own*, she thought. Besides, they were young. They would have another when the time was right. But not now. Not now. The thoughts put a spring in her step as she reached the plaza before the church where the couple agreed to meet.

Selene noticed the only slouched figure on the corner right away, and she knew it was Marcos by his long neck and wide shoulders. Through the late-night garúa, through the chilly evening mist, she could see her boyfriend staring up at the illuminated statue of the Magdalene, the patron saint of Casma, encased in glass above the church entrance. She made her way across the street. Reaching Marcos, Selene could hear him slightly sobbing.

"Marcos?"

He didn't look her way. Instead, his gaze stayed on the Magdalene. On the skull in her hand. The skull of a small child.

"What's wrong?"

He sobbed even harder. Selene turned him around to face her. Sand sprinkled his face and hair. And pressed against his bloodied chest, Marcos held Hércules tight.

"I..." he slowly let out, and he fell to his knees.

Selene touched his face. She thumbed Marcos' sandy tears. She pressed his face against her belly where tiny jolts surprised her from the inside. And they stood there beneath the saint, before the weeping church doors, wondering about tomorrow.

utero

Caligula Pérez

I met Marcos in early March that year, not long before the rain finally came.

I was standing in front of my open locker, a newbie who could care less about the new high school, when a tug on my elbow sent my notebook to the floor.

"You Ha-Jaime, right?"

"Yeah," I shot back, annoyed.

The warning bell rang. On the way back up I caught the scuffed Sketchers, the black chinos and long-sleeved shirt, the pen stuck behind his ear. It didn't take long for me to recognize the same short, thick-jawed local that sat behind me in Miss Cavazos's Advanced History 101.

"I got class," I said to him, and flipped my locker shut.

"Leh-Let's go, then," he said, and he cut into the long hallway already thinning of other teenage bodies. Then I'm not sure why, but something made me follow him. Maybe I felt sorry for his stutter. Maybe it had something to do with being new and not pussying out. Or maybe deep down somewhere I needed a friend, even a puny one like Marcos. I don't know. But whatever it was, it made me catch up with him, all the way to the bathroom where Marcos forearmed the door and let me through.

The room reeked of piss. Marcos checked under all the stalls before locking the door.

"Miss C's qwa-quiz," he bungled out, backing into the grimy tiles between the urinals. "You got the A. After only a week. How?"

The entire room went into auto flush. I lied and told him I'd taken a class covering Ancient Rome before, the biggies, from Julius Caesar to Augustus. The final bell rang. A fist pounded outside the door a few times. Marcos pushed off the wall and came straight at me.

"Your number, quick!" he demanded, and before I knew it, I was giving Marcos my ten digits. He wrote them down fast on the palm of his hand. He took my notebook and scribbled inside it. He gave it back before rushing out the door.

The fist outside turned out to be Felix, another guy from Miss Cavazos's. He ran in and zipped open and let his piss go. "Why the fuck you assholes lock the door, huh?" I opened my notebook and turned to the page where everything written, including MARCOS PÉREZ, was in all caps.

Home those days meant the stink of sardines and coffee pretty much all day.

It meant holding my breath every morning while getting ready for school. It meant my convict-turned-preacher uncle at the kitchen table all day, flicking bits of Premium crackers off the handwritten pages of his next sermon. "My bitter wine, my process," he explained to me and Mom the night we arrived. He had a tattoo of a teardrop on the outside of his left eye that Mom warned me never to ask him about. He soothed his throat with a few loud sips from his favorite mug, the one the prison had given him with JESUS SAVES in big black letters. Mom balanced a spoonful of sugar over her own cup. "I just think of our Lord on his cross," he carried on, "determined to save humanity, with nothing to drink but sour wine from a sponge on a spear. Matthew 24:48."

Mom dumped the sugar back into the jar.

"'Sacrifice to Salvation,'" my uncle said. "That's my motto. That's what you'll get at my church. You'll see it all Saturday." He eyed us both, especially me, then back at Mom. "Now, give me the key and stay inside the house until I'm back. Got it?"

I didn't say a word; Mom handed the key over. Her lip still fat, she sipped her coffee black, exactly how she hated it.

"And how about today?" my uncle bothered me in the present. He held a cracker with those shiny chunks of fish flesh again. "Got homework," I answered back, turning him down like each day before. I had one foot in the hallway when Mom came into the kitchen.

"Homework again, Hermanita," my uncle said to her. "Just like yesterday, and the day before that, and the day before that. Let's get started, then."

"In a minute, Dámaso." She poured herself some coffee. Except for her lip, her face seemed to loosen up when her eyes fell on me. "Did you have a good day at school?"

"The best," I said, watching the cracker and dismembered sardine disappear behind my uncle's lips.

"I'm just asking."

"I've got homework."

"That's it?"

"Let him go, Margarita."

"Why won't you talk to me?"

"I don't want to talk."

"Why not?"

"Let me go!"

"Margarita!"

By the time my uncle pulled Mom off of me her coffee was all over the floor. She ran out the side door. After glaring at me in a silence that stunk with everything in his mouth, my uncle finally followed her out the door, too.

I headed for my room. When they came back in, I heard him insisting he was calm, that he wasn't losing his nerve one bit, so stop it. That she'd come to him, remember, not the other way around. That everything he'd done for us—the bike, the new cell phones—meant nothing would ever be the same again, ever. For once, I agreed with him. Then the praying started. A soft sunlight peeked under the door to my room. I punched in and drew the shades to make the room dark.

When you come, César, it's after school and I'm standing in front of our apartment complex in Huntington Park. Chato's bike is the chrome beast with the leather saddle parked on the curb. The handlebars poke up and out like horns. On the gas tank, where the Harley logo should be, there's an airbrushed eagle with outspread wings. I don't want to look at it anymore, but I don't want to go inside either.

It's a quarter past five and I can still smell the fresh rolls from the corner bakery. Across the street a group of kids play hopscotch on the sidewalk. When Mom stumbles out the front gate her lip is a mess, a smashed rose.

She staggers past me, jumps on the beast, and starts the engine.
"Get on!"
"What?"
"Get on!!!"
"Why?"
"Please!"
"Fine!!!"
I climb on behind her. By the time a bloody-eyed Chato bursts through the gate the mufflers drown out everything he is yelling. The kids are scrambling. Mom's hair slaps my face through the getaway air; I press my cheek to hers, hold on tight. She speeds up at every yellow light so she doesn't have to stop. And it isn't until we're well past Blythe and into the Arizona saguaros that she stops to feed the beast and tells me what happened.

MY HOUSE IN 15 is what the text read.

I opened the curtains and reached for my notebook to make sure. By then, my uncle was in review mode in the kitchen, reminding Mom about the proper temperature for the pool water. No, he said, promising her that everyone would cry *Hallelujah!* in welcome, embrace the pastor's own sister with joyful arms. "You'll see it all Saturday," he said matter-of-factly. "Jaime, too." That briny smell invaded my room again. "Amen," he declared. I typed the address into Maps. "Amen," Mom repeated. I opened the window and climbed out.

For an ex-city slicker like me, my uncle's neighborhood left a lot to be desired. Outside his house the scene repeated itself no matter where I looked: the same thin streets dipping into chain-link fences on both sides. Mesquite trees everywhere. Wild shrubs growing out of old toilets or semi tires. On most porches, steel drums-turned-barbeque pits and decorated with Dallas Cowboys' Lonestars. And sidewalks or street signs, they hadn't been invented in this part of the world, apparently. Cutting through the streets with my phone before me, I felt like a nomad to all the old ladies hosing the late-day dust off their front porches.

I finally found the address stickered onto a crooked mailbox up to its neck in brush. A patch of dirt led up to an old trailer, and next to that, a beat-up wooden shed. The sun sat on its roof, ready to fall into the other side of the world.

"Come on!" Marcos waved at me from behind a half-torn screen door. A dog barked somewhere, followed by others, and I wondered why they hadn't noticed me before. "Hurry up!" he called again, so I shuffled up the steps. He ushered me into a small, dimly lit room that was nothing more than a couch on old carpet, the windows all covered up in aluminum foil. On a tray in a corner a few candles burned. The flames leaned back up when Marcos closed the door behind me.

"He's almost here," he said with hardly a stutter.

"Who?"

"Just watch."

"What the fuck's going on?"

"Here he cuh-comes."

The oven of that room tortured the tips of my elbows first, then the back of my neck and throat. I swallowed but nothing moist went down. The dogs really went at it when the loud corrido and mufflers blared outside. Then it all died when a heavy door slammed shut.

The man who walked in owned the same thick jaw as Marcos. He wore camouflage all the way down to dirty boots and gripped a rifle in one hand, a pair of dead rabbits in the other. Standing there looking at us, he seemed to belong to that trailer more than everything in it, including Marcos. And something told me that if the walls around us could have found some way to come together to form a throat, that man would have been the one to choke the life right out of it.

"The fuck is this?" the man said.

"Cuh-candles. The Ruh-Romans did it in their tuh-temples."

"I could give two fucks about that."

"My fuh-friend, Jaime. We got the same last name."

The man's eyes stuffed a spear deep into me. I didn't dare speak. He leaned the rifle against the side of the couch. He sat himself down, dropped the bloodied rabbits on his lap, and spread his arms along the backrest.

"He's leaving now," Marcos said.

"No," the man said. He stretched out his legs, dug his heels into the dirty carpet. "Not yet."

"Ernesto, puh-please."

"Now," Ernesto said, "in front of him, or else…"

And Marcos did as he was told while I got to watch. He knelt in front of Ernesto and began to unlace the left boot, then the right. He grabbed hold of the heels and pulled until the boots came off and set them both at the foot of the couch.

"Good boy," Ernesto said, then he kicked Marcos straight in his chest. He towed his legs in as Marcos gasped for air. He fisted the rabbit ears with one hand. "Now come get 'em," he said, "and don't forget the beer."

Marcos picked himself up slowly. He took the rabbits and staggered past me, still catching his breath, until I couldn't see him anymore.

POP! went Ernesto's thumb from the rifle's muzzle.

I didn't wait for Marcos to come back. I rushed out the screen door and into a night loud with the barks and snarls of *Get out!* but *Please, don't go.*

"He died under mysterious circumstances," Miss Cavazos shared with the class.

Her voice vaulted off the whiteboard as she markered TIBERIUS 14AD-37AD in a thick red. Her thin wrists went perfectly with her voice and frame. I penciled the name and dates in my notebook waiting for Marcos to walk through the door.

"Suetonius claims," Miss Cavazos continued, "that Macro, Captain of the Praetorian Guard, smothered Emperor Tiberius in his sleep. Another historian, Tacitus, asserts that he was poisoned by his nephew, Gaius Caesar, more famously known as Caligula. You should remember that name." She faced the class and looked at us through her wide-framed glasses. "And that, ladies and gentlemen, is where our first episode begins. Any questions before the video starts?"

"Miss, yeah," sounded Felix from his desk by the window. "So you're saying this Cali-culo guy, he killed the Tiburón guy? Is that it?" He turned to look at me. "Did it happen in the bathroom, Miss, with the door locked?"

The class erupted into laughter. Felix flipped me off under the bad acne on his chin. I turned to Miss Cavazos again. Like the statue on her desk of the Capitoline Wolf getting her nipples jerked by Romulus and Remus, she didn't even flinch. "The lights, Susie," she seemed to growl, and the room went dark. "And you, Felix—LET'S GO!" and she marched him out of the room to a chorus of oohs.

All of a sudden, the large screen above Miss Cavazos's desk bathed everyone in a blue light, settling the class back down. A dull mosaic floor appeared at first. Then cymbals crashed, followed by zany flutes and horns, until a checkered viper slithered across the phrase I, CLAVDIVS, inlaid into the mosaic in Classical Roman script.

When class let out, I found Marcos leaning against my locker door. He looked a mess, the same clothes, his shoulders slumped up to his ears.

"Your nuh-notes," he said, counting all of the feet rushing by him.

I surrendered my notebook and watched him walk away.

It's New Year's Eve now, César, and you're forcing me to watch HBO's Rome again. Centurion Titus Pullo is sparring with the young Octavian, the future Emperor Augustus, all because Atia his mother says it's time to learn to do the things men do. They're using wooden swords and shields. When you come back in you slam the door behind you. I catch enough of the music and voices outside to know Chato and Mom and their friends are having a blast.

After you toss me a Coke, you crack yours open, drink. Instead of sitting next to me you stand by your desk, restless. When the scene cuts to Atia fucking Timon the Jew, you don't tell me to lower the volume this time. We both watch and listen as Atia rides Timon like a wild beast and climaxes loud.

"I'm leaving, Little Brother."

"But the bakery's closed, César."

"No. I'm leaving for a while. I want you to know first."

"Where?"

"Europe. For the whole semester. To help my professor with his research. We leave in a couple of days."

I hit PAUSE with Atia still on top, and ask, "But what about Mom?"

"Take care of her."

"And Chato?"

"I'm going to talk to her about that piece of shit before I go."

"And, me?"

You take another sip. On the other side of the door the muffled cheers are getting louder.

"Look, I'll bring you back a chunk of the Colosseum, I promise, Little Brother. And when I'm a professor you can show it off to all my classes. Deal?"

I don't say anything and press PLAY instead. It's back to Pullo and Octavian again, this time lunging at each other with real swords.

You finally sit down next to me. At the stroke of midnight even the gun shots and fireworks and police sirens can't drown out the squawkers and party horns on the other side of the door. When you put your arm around me, I let you.

"Oh, and I'm not gonna call either, Little Brother. I'm gonna write to you, okay? Just like the Romans did, they wrote letters, so we're gonna do that, too. Deal?"

I raise the volume all the way up to hear the cold hard steel crash.

My uncle's unnamed church was a hole in the wall in a corner strip, across from Shuko Kai Karate.

He unlocked the glass door, turned on the lights, and pointed to a folding chair just inside. "You wait here, Jaime," he said. "Like I told you: When they come in, say Hello! or Hola! or Welcome, Brothers and Sisters!—just like that. They'll gather here for a little, then find their seats when the music starts. Come on." He led Mom up a few rows of chairs to a small stage with a drum set and instruments on the right, a blue kiddie pool on the left. Behind that, a large white cross suspended above red curtains. He found the partition and led Mom through. I heard the car brakes and muffled slams of car doors behind me. Through the tinted glass the cars all parked in a gloom, it seemed, just like the bodies that escaped them.

I avoided eye contact each time I let someone new in, and I never said Hello or Hola. Before long the lobby was crowded with young and old bodies mixing English and Spanish loud, hand-shaking and cheek-kissing and -pinching in their Saturday best. What was odd was I couldn't spot anyone close to my age, not even in the band members plugging in instruments on the stage. As parents and grandparents bounced even more God-filled phrases off each other, the children stood transfixed along the glass on both sides of the door. Along with me, they watched the black-and-white movie outside, starring our luckier counterparts, all of them running for the dojo in their white uniforms. I shook a new hand, let whoever it was in. In the last open spot in front of the church a group of boys took turns showing off their roundhouse kicks. Another hand, another body inside. The boys finally moved out of the way to let a white Range Rover park.

The fat man who climbed out of that truck wore cowboy boots under a purple suit and tie. I saw scalp beneath his thin hair. He headed straight for me, the grin on his face doing nothing to keep me from locking the door. But I opened it, shook his fat hand when he poked it in.

"How's it going, boy? Where's Dámaso?"

"Who knows."

"Ha! Your uncle mentioned your Christian spirit!"

He swung the door open but stood in the frame. The outside heat began to suck out the cool air. He still wouldn't move. Several families gathered behind him, all of them sweating to get in, but no one protested. They seemed content to suffer beneath the sun, switching Bibles from one sweaty hand to the other, just as the band's first breaths of life sounded from the stage.

"Ah, Don Tiberio! Bienvenido! Come in, come in!"

My uncle shook the fat man's hand and finally pulled him inside. The families wasted no time filing in.

"What do you think?" my uncle asked, gesturing over the chairs and onto the stage where Mom carefully poured a pitcherful of water into the pool.

"Oh, yes. Fine, fine," the fat man said.

"You'll sit up front. I'll call you up at the end of the sermon. Margarita will be next to you. She knows what to do."

Mom slipped back through the curtains. My uncle and the fat man laughed. The band settled on a tune everyone began singing along to. Parents pried their children from the glass and began leading them to the chairs.

"A real pleasure, boy," the fat man said. "We can talk some more after, I'm sure," and he followed my uncle in.

Alone in that lobby I couldn't think of any reason to stay. The first few bars of *Amazing Grace* pulled on my ears. A voice that could only belong to the fat man started on the first verse, then "Go, Margarita, go!" my uncle insisted, over and over, until Mom joined in. The congregation cheered. I kicked the door open and sucked in a long breath of the muggy air on my way out.

I zigzagged between the cars in their brightest colors, the hard sun making sure of that over the slow drum from the morning traffic. I pulled on the knot in my tie over the knot in my throat and undid my shirt button when CLANG! The ping of metal rang hard on the asphalt somewhere. I turned to my left and right over all of the windshield glares until I caught sight of a well-dressed woman not too far away. Clutching a white purse, she busied herself talking down to the driver-side tire of a black sedan.

"Germanicus, yes. Born 15 BC, died 19AD. Drusus the Elder was his father." The string of names and dates came out aggravated from that familiar voice. "Are you sure you don't need to lift the car off the ground first?"

"Yes," the other voice said. "What about his wuh-wife?"

"Agrippina, daughter of Augustus. You know, if you'd come to class, you'd have all of this down. Why were you absent again?"

No answer. Miss Cavazos looked at her watch.

"It's ten till and that's not working," she said. "I really have to go."

"Agripee-Agripee," Marcos kept trying.

"Just leave it alone. I'll call Triple A."

"Okay, Miss." Marcos stood up with the tire iron in his hand. "But tell me about Cuh-Caligula. Please?"

"Can I help?" I said, and when Miss Cavazos turned to face me, I almost didn't recognize her. She wore an elegant white dress with matching pumps, the complete opposite of her jeans and t-shirt school image. Her black hair flowed down around her glasses, covered her ears now, and curled into her lean neck. She looked way younger in all her makeup and red lipstick, even though at school everyone said she was closer to twenty-five.

"Jaime? What are you doing here?"

"Church is his uncle's," Marcos said without a hitch.

"Really? Then you know—Has the service started yet?"

"Almost," I answered, wondering what on earth she had to do in my uncle's church. She had small, well-manicured hands. I took the tire iron from Marcos. "You should hurry," I said. "I'll take care of this for you."

"But in your shirt and tie? No, Jaime. I can call Triple A."

"We got this, Miss," Marcos reassured her.

"Yeah," I said. "We do. It's okay. Go."

She looked us both over, checked her watch again. "Okay," she finally said. "Thank you both. I'll see you inside in a bit, then." I nodded. "And Marcos: I expect to see you in class Monday. No more absences." She turned and went through the cars and was gone.

"Jack first, smartass," I snapped at Marcos.

He nodded and took the tire iron from me. He slipped it into the jack and began pumping up and down. I rolled up my sleeves and pulled the spare from the trunk.

"You know," I said, "it's one thing to invite me to your house. But following me here?"

He didn't respond. He finished with the jack and started on the nuts. I dropped the spare next to him and watched him lean in and pull and huff until one by one the nuts and tire came off. He moved out of the way to let me roll the spare on. I made sure everything was tight before letting the air out of the jack.

After putting everything away, we walked to the corner store and bought two Dasanis to cool off. We sat in silence and drank on the curb as the cars rolled by. Marcos stared up at a jet cutting through the sky. When I finally finished rehearsing what I wanted to say to him after class the other day, he stood straight up.

"Come on," he said.

We made it about a block down to a small park where a man in a suit jumped from his table to offer us copies of *The Watchtower*. I followed Marcos's lead and ran faster than him under all the mesquite trees, all the way to a spot of grass in front of a wide circle of white columns. The stone felt warm beneath that relentless sun. When Marcos finally caught up, he walked through the columns like he'd seen it all before.

I went through the columns too. Marcos stood with his chin tucked into his throat, staring hard into an amphitheater that sunk down into nine concentric circles.

"The other night," he said clearly. "You saw."

My phone vibrated—WHERE R U???—and I glared into the last circle of all, the stage.

"Sorry...I, I gotta go," I said.

He sighed, then nodded. He unscrewed the lid off his Dasani, poured what was left on his head. He sat down on the step, the water dripping off his nose as I left him there.

Three quarters through the parking lot the church door burst open. I stopped and hung from the branch of a crape myrtle. The fat man wore a white towel around his neck now, my uncle's hand on his right shoulder. They walked out together with the entire assembly behind them and singing *Las Mañanitas* at the tops of their lungs. One by one, old and young, they all took turns congratulating the fat man, then scrambled to their cars for the air conditioning. Mom walked out with Miss Cavazos. Side by side, anyone could easily confuse them for sisters, even mother and daughter. A bird shuffled in the leaves above me. I left the shade and made for the last line of cars in front of the church.

"Glad you could make it!" my uncle said, his eyes telling a different story.

"Congratulations," I said to the fat man, shaking his hand.

"Thanks, boy." He took the cigarette from his lips and wiped his face with the towel.

"Where were you?" Mom demanded. "And your tie and shirt—what happened?"

"Don't be mad at him, please," Miss Cavazos jumped in. "They helped change my flat tire."

"They?" Mom turned to her. The fat man released the smoke from his chest, then nodded when my uncle pointed above the door where the name of the church was supposed to be.

"Jaime and Marcos," Miss Cavazos explained. "They're my students, believe it or not. Both of them." One more look at me and Mom and she finally put it all together. "Oh, you must be Jaime's mother. I—"

"Jessica!" the fat man shouted.

"Just a second, Dad."

"Now, Jessica!"

Miss Cavazos pursed her lips, a bit embarrassed. "Okay, Dad," she finally said, then offered Mom her hand. "Nice meeting you. And I'll see you Monday, Jaime. Goodbye."

Through my shock my uncle just lathered it on: "And God bless you, Don Tiberio! And you too, Jessica! It's going to look fantastic up there, you'll see! I'll call you Monday with an update."

"No," said the fat man. He dropped what was left of his cigarette to the asphalt. "Margarita's stopping by. We worked it out already. Send the update with her."

"Yes, Tiberio," Mom said. "We'll be there Monday night, don't worry."

I nearly snapped my neck turning to Mom.

"Take care of your mother for me, boy," the fat man said. He tossed his towel at me. Miss Cavazos got into the Range Rover and they drove away.

My uncle headed back inside. I let the towel fall to the ground.

"She's nice," Mom said to me. "Pretty, too. What's she teach?"

When I failed to answer her, she picked up the towel and disappeared through the door.

A lone cloud smeared thin over the spot where the fat man stopped to let Miss Cavazos out. She got in her sedan and drove off. When the doors to Shuko Kai opened not a single boy or girl rushed out. A broad-shouldered Asian man, in full uniform and black belt, came out instead.

"History..." I whispered under my breath.

The man bowed towards the sun. "Hai!" he cried loud, his perfect thrust kick all heel and sole.

"All south from here," Mom says to me. "Four more hours if we just keep going."

It's late at night along I-10 on the outskirts of San Antonio when she climbs off to pump because she knows I won't do it. Her hair is a mess, she's still not wearing a bra. She stuffs a twenty in my hand and tells me to go inside and pay. My back and legs are stiff after three states, my eyes dry from all the wind, the crying. I don't look the guy behind the counter in the face. When I'm back outside there's a truck parked under the Texaco star. The driver is kicking mud off his tires, and I know it's all just to look at Mom. The beast with gigantic antlers is tied to his hood and bleeding down the front grill.

And my thoughts are stuck on you, César, when the man's first cat call comes—HEY, WHAT'S YOUR NAME, SWEETHEART? The woman's name is Marzia from Rome and she isn't on the phone long before she starts crying. The professor and the embassy guy do most of the talking. YEAH, KILLED IT 'BOUT AN HOUR AGO. FUCKER NEARLY ESCAPED, BUT I GOT HIS ASS. After explaining what happened they tell Mom they're sorry. That the police searched far and wide for over a week but never found any trace of your body. THAT LIP SURE LOOKS BAD. WHERE Y'ALL STAYING TONIGHT? Mom gets up off the living room floor, doesn't even hang up the phone. She goes into her bedroom where Chato is asleep and reaches for his keys. "Where you think you're going?" he says getting up, and punches her on the mouth when she resists. She tells me she thought of nothing but you when she put the key in Chato's eye and ran away. YOUR BOY? NAH, NAH. DON'T WORRY 'BOUT HIM. HE CAN WAIT IN MY TRUCK, C'MON. WE'LL BE INSIDE. WATTA YOU SAY?

Mom finally spots me coming her way. "I can't," she tells the tire kicker, pulls up her blouse, hangs the pump back up.

"Dumb bitch," the man shoots back, and heads for the store.

I climb on behind Mom and lock my fingers just under her sagging breasts, the engine spitting and sputtering. Under all the beast's blood, the truck's grill is a punched grin.

"All south from here," Mom says again.

I know, I don't say out loud, I know, the tears rolling down my face.

Monday morning started when I couldn't tell the difference between Miss Cavazos and the chalk-white she-wolf on her desk, still stuck suckling Romulus and Remus.

It didn't start earlier with my nightmare of Ernesto grunting outside the window, either, then storming in to chop me up and stuff me into sardine cans for my uncle's pleasure. Not in the car with Mom going on and on about the fat man's success. Not with the sight of Marcos's desk empty yet again. It began instead with a pale-faced Miss Cavazos standing in front of the screen in her regular jeans and spirit shirt again, the taste of something like sardines in my own mouth, as I tried to rip from my brain who her father was.

"Caligula became emperor," she started all of a sudden, "and he immediately proclaimed himself the god Jove. That's Zeus in Greek mythology, by the way. He declared his favorite sister, Drusilla, a goddess as well. That's where we left off Friday. Questions?"

"Miss, yes." It was Felix again after a short silence. "I have one: I read online this Cali-culo dude slept with his sister. That she even had his baby. That true?"

The girls in class gasped, then giggled.

Miss Cavazos's eyes finally found me; her face flushed red. The screen went blue again. She turned off the lights and rushed out the door.

All around me smart phones shimmered to laughter. On the large screen a group of Roman senators groveled at the feet of Caligula-turned-Jove. Felix snorted from his desk. The sun outside threatened to burst through the blinds like some Roman galley heading straight for the classroom at ramming speed. I stood up and made for the door.

Miss Cavazos stood cross-armed in the empty hallway. She stared deep into the trophy display just outside the teachers' lounge.

"Miss Cavazos?"

"Go back inside, please."

"You all right?"

"Fine, fine. Just go."

She pressed her elbows onto the glass. I looked everywhere to make sure no one was around.

"Look, it's weird, I get it. But what can we do? You want me out of your class?"

"No," she said.

"Then what?"

She didn't respond. Her fascination looking through the glass started to annoy me, until I had to see for myself. Under a banner reading SPARTAN PRIDE sat a collection of trophies and plaques decorated with red and gold ribbons. Etched onto the gold plate on the biggest trophy of all was

GIRLS PENTATHLON 2012
JESSICA CAVAZOS
FIRST PLACE

The janitor lady rolled out of the teachers' bathroom, the job done.

"Marcos," Miss Cavazos finally said, still with her back to me. "He's absent again today. You know, I really wanted to thank him."

I waited for her to turn around, but she didn't. When I walked back into class all eyes were stuck to the screen. Even Felix stared up open-mouthed. Crazy-eyed Caligula-turned-Jove held in front of him the child he'd just cut from Drusilla's womb.

Then he ate it.

In the kitchen that afternoon I grabbed the two bacon and egg tacos from the stove.

The sardine-coffee smell was faint, the table empty, so I knew my uncle was out. I took the milk out of the fridge. With Caligula still eating in my mind I made it through the first few bites. It wasn't long before Mom hurried in, in the same dress she'd worn to church. Her hair was pulled back into a neat ponytail this time. With all the makeup and lipstick, even where Chato had hit her, I had to look real close to find anything there.

"So? I don't have another dress."

"Good," I said flatly. I took a drink straight from the carton.

"Just 'good'?"

"I'm eating."

She waited near the sink in silence.

"Whatever. Let's go," I said, and I stuffed the milk back in the fridge on my way out.

In the car I rolled my tongue over my teeth and swallowed the last bits of bacon, egg, and tortilla. Neither of us said a word. Mom flipped on the Christian station she liked to listen to now. The world outside wasted no time transforming into the busier side of town with all the boulevards and Whataburgers. "Ha-lle-lu-jah!" Mom sang under her breath, and my thoughts like those streets began passing me by and mixing all together: Finding out about César, of course. Marcos and those rabbits. Miss Cavazos sprinting, hurdling, vaulting onto the platform to claim her prize. "Ha-lle-lu-jah!" Caligula-turned-Jove, taking his last bite. "Ha-lle-lu-jah!" and the song finished. A man's voice took over, offering an inspirational quote with the Bible verses to go with it.

Mom parked and killed the guy off. She pulled down the visor and looked in the mirror.

"I look okay?" she asked again. I didn't respond. She flipped up the visor and got out of the car.

The door to *Don Tiberio's Christian Gifts* led into cooler air that smelled of candle wax more than anything. Past the register tall shelves lined the walls with every religious item you could think of, big and small, from rosaries to small statues of saints to thick Bibles of all colors. There was even a section for kids with a couch and rug and a small TV looping a muted animation of the life of Saint Peter with subtitles. Hanging on the walls were crosses of all sizes and paintings of Jesus blessing and bleeding. The small notecards below listed the prices in both American dollars and Mexican pesos.

The center of the room was split in two. On the left you had long racks labeled BAPTISM and FIRST COMMUNION, lined with suits and dresses wrapped in transparent plastic. On the right, more shelves but stuffed with shoe boxes. A lone boy sat on a stool frowning as a chubby woman crammed a shiny black shoe onto his foot. I caught the long-winded breathing long before the fat man appeared around a corner shelf and stopped next to the boy.

"Try this one," the fat man said.

He handed the woman a new shoe from the box he was carrying, similar to the three already scattered around her. She put it on the boy, pinched the tip to feel for his toes. She nodded. "Good," the fat man said. "Smart of you to buy them for your boy early, Pilar." He put the shoe back in the box. "Before the summer rush, I mean. I'll charge you over here," and he led the woman to the register.

While the register clacked and pinged, Mom decided to help the boy put his shoes back on. When she finished, she put the rest of the shoes in their boxes and stacked them neatly on top of each other.

"Help your mother, boy," the fat man shouted to me all the way from the register.

I picked up the boxes. The boy ran to his mother and out the door they went.

"'Employees Only.' You see that door? You take that in there and wait for me. Your mom and I need to talk. Got it?"

Rather than give Mom the eyes she expected I just did as I was told and headed for the door in the back wall. A short corridor led me into a poorly lit space stacked with large cardboard boxes. A lone table cut through the center of the room, filled with broken statues, picture frames, rosaries, shoes and other trinkets. But none of this mess mattered, I remembered. As my uncle had put it, there was always going to be collateral damage in any war worth fighting. And all of life is a war, he assured me and Mom. In his own case it meant overcoming his past and doing anything and everything, no matter the cost, to make sure his church thrived. For the fat man, all the broken merchandise represented his price paid for six stores, including the one I was in, spread out over three counties. I rested the boxes on the table and wondered what my part in all these wars could be. Some great Roman dux, perhaps, with all the battle scars to prove it, commanding my legions down from the rafters to burn everything down.

My legions scrambled back into the shadows immediately when I heard someone shuffling in. It was Miss Cavazos. She wasn't wearing her glasses, though, and her hair was pulled back. She wore a thin red sweater with matching leggings and sneakers. Headphones looped around the back of her neck.

"They're gone, Jaime," she said, slightly out of breath. "He sent me in to tell you. He was hungry, you see, so he closed early and they went to dinner. He said you should be fine walking home."

"I'll see you later," I snapped, moving past her, preparing to summon my legions to ransack every shelf in the store.

"Wait," she said; I stopped. "Since you're here, before you go, let me show you something. It won't take long. Come on."

She moved to a darker spot between two stacks of boxes and opened a door. She flicked on the lights. Tall stone columns lined up against the white walls. At the far end of the small room stood a marble fountain with a life-sized statue of a woman inside it. Her head cocked up slightly, she looked into the recessed lights with stone eyes. One hand gripped her toga, while the other greeted me with an open palm.

"He rents all this out to weddings, quinceañeras, stuff like that. Not her, though. She's what I wanted to show you. She's the Sibyl. The famous oracle from ancient times. I covered her in class before you arrived. As the story goes, she was given to Apollo as a child. He grew so fond of her he gave her the gift of prophecy, they say. After that, only the most worthy were allowed to receive her knowledge for a thousand years."

With the columns closing in, Miss Cavazos gazed at that pale, smooth face as if waiting for the Sibyl to speak.

"This morning, Jaime...the way I acted...I..."

I waited for her to finish. She blushed and began to ramble in retreat instead. "Yes, okay. Never mind. We're covering Ancient Rome and this room just reminds me of that and I thought I'd show you, that's all. This is stupid, so stupid. We should go. We should go."

She turned off the lights and sent the Sibyl back into the blackest of holes.

Outside the night air felt soggy. Miss Cavazos found her helmet and put it on, unchained her bike from the rack.

"I'll see you tomorrow, then," she said, climbing on. She rested her right sneaker on the pedal but wouldn't leave.

"She belonged to my mother, you know," she finally said. "A wedding gift, from my father. We kept the statue in our backyard. When I was a little girl, I liked jumping into the fountain in the summertime. The Sibyl would tell me things that always came true. But when Mom died, she didn't tell me. I swore never to speak to her again. I couldn't even look at her after that. She's been in that room ever since. Good night."

I waved at her as she rode away. When my phone vibrated, I just knew it wasn't Mom.

It's New Year's Day, César, and Mom's passed out on the couch when you tell me it's time. Lying on her side, she's in nothing but panties and a bra. One hand rests on her hip; the arm beneath is bent and ends palm up. You kick through the beer cans and ciga- rette butts to wake her up.

"Here," you say, tossing her a blanket. "We have to talk."

And you tell her you're leaving and why. That Little Brother already knows.

"Don't..." she slurs, wrapping the blanket around her. She can barely sit up.

"Then promise me he won't come back here anymore. Promise that and I won't go."

"Don't..."

"Promise that!"

And you're shaking her shoulders and crying "YOU DUMB BITCH!" when Chato storms through the front door and pins you up against the wall, hard.

"Don't..." Mom slavers again before falling back on the couch, palms up.

And I can't move.

By the time I turned into Marcos's street I was already a sweaty mess. In the dark every porch resembled a black hole. Once again, the dogs paid no attention to me. I reached the mailbox. At the foot of the steps Marcos was rustling through some pages.

"What's that?"

"Ruh-reading your notes."

"In the dark?"

"Better this way."

I blew air through my teeth, kicked some dirt. I searched up high for stars that quickly transformed into constellations of the fat man grinning and leaning across the table to feed Mom an appetizer. Of Miss Cavazos jumping into her fountain for a new secret from the Sibyl. Of César, just before the beast took all of him away.

The mufflers roared around the corner first, then the high beams lit up the street. The loud corrido woke all the dogs again. Porch lights came on, went off. The headlights swerved into the drive and hit Marcos first. Holding my notebook to his chest, his face was a collection of dark bruises.

The music died; the dogs and headlights didn't. Ernesto climbed out of the truck with his rifle again.

"Well, well," he said. "You two still like it in the dark, eh?" He was the only one who laughed. "Tsss. Get the back, then. You and your friend here. And don't fuck up the ribs. You know how Dámaso likes them. Turn off the lights when you're finished, or else."

He buried something hard into Marcos's chest and stomped up the steps.

Marcos gave me my notebook back. Before I could ask what other jobs he or Ernesto did for my uncle he climbed into the back of the truck. He turned on a small flashlight. Lying on a tarp was the largest mass of the thickest black hair and hooves I'd ever seen. The smell made me gag. Dead on its side, with its snout and tusks hanging over a pool of blood, one yellow eye stared directly at me.

"We buh-buried the bike," Marcos said, looking down at the beast. "No one's ever guh-gonna find you or your Mom."

"What are you talking about?"

"You owe me."

"You're fucking crazy!"

Marcos breathed loud through his nose. He put the flashlight between his teeth and crouched down. He used a pocket knife to slice off both of the beast's ears at the base of the skull. He stood up tall and as straight as ever and hurled the ears as far as he could, up and over the trailer, where I was sure the dogs would devour them soon enough.

"Just grab it, then," he snapped, his voice breaking. The coarse hair around the beast's thick ankles wasn't one but every nail ever made, and hammered deep.

Days later I still couldn't get that smell off my hands.

I hung over the kitchen faucet again, lathered up to my elbows, scrubbing until my skin turned red. But it was no use. I thought of texting Marcos, but didn't. I dried off. The stench on me was worse than the disemboweled sardine can on the counter, the knife to blame right next to the coffeemaker.

"Margarita!" My uncle rushed into the kitchen. "Come here, quick!" He set his plate and mug on the counter, spread out the large white sheet on the table with both hands.

He didn't look at me, and I was fine with that. He blinked over the architectural plans filled with overlapping rectangles. The largest one of all, the one at the center with SACRIFICE TO SALVATION in big block letter, included a wide-winged dove swinging in from below.

Mom came in. The new dress the fat man had bought her was a red one, low cut, and tight around the knees. On her feet she wore what she called "gladiator" sandals. Her hair was up again, the makeup even heavier, her lip all but healed.

"Here, look," my uncle said, a finger pointed above the dove's head. "Don Tiberio wasn't sure when I showed this to him last night. Will it be the verse from Paul or Peter?"

"I'll ask him when I get there, Dámaso. It's already late." She looked at me. "Ready?"

"Tell him to call me right away, Margarita. This goes up Saturday morning, right before your baptism. I need to let the shop know. Don't forget."

He grabbed his plate and mug and sucked and chomped over the most important thing to him in the world. I grabbed my backpack and followed Mom out the door.

Outside the sky was gray and the air smelled of grass. In the car I took out my notebook so I didn't have to speak. She didn't flip on the radio. When she turned at the empty lot, I knew right away why she'd offered to drive me to school on her way to work.

CIRCUS MAXIMUS—ROME'S CHARIOT RACING STADIUM

"She asked about you, Jessica, your teacher. Did you know she used to be a pretty good athlete?"

VOMITORIUM—NOT WHERE ROMANS VOMITTED, IT'S THE ENTRANCE TO THE COLOSSEUM

"Tiberio will be there Saturday. You know that, right? He thinks you don't like him. He likes you a lot."

CHIEF VESTAL: WOMEN THAT GUARDED THE SECRET FIRE OF VESTA THAT SYMBOLIZED ROME

"At least look at me, Jaime!"

INCITATUS: CALIGULA'S HORSE-TURNED-SENATOR; HAD HIS OWN SERVANTS AND A GOLD BUCKET FOR WATER

"It wasn't my fault! When people want to leave, you can't stop them! I'm still here. Why won't you look at me?"

ROSTRA VETERA: PLATFORM WHERE SENATORS DELIVERED SPEECHES

The first drops of rain splashed hard on the windshield.

"It's never rained here much, except for hurricanes," Mom sighed. "All I remember about growing up here is the thirst." She wrapped both palms on the steering wheel. "Your father left when it rained. César was five, you were still inside me. He said he was tired of the wild pigs digging under our fence whenever it rained.

Of the grunting outside late at night, begging him to let the beast through the door."

DAMNATIO AD BESTIAS, THE CONDEMNATION TO BEASTS, I read, and that riotous audience in the Colosseum of my head cheered as the beast of all beasts ripped into flesh and cracked through bones.

She pulled a crumpled envelope from her purse. "Here," she said, and handed it to me. "This came the day we left. I thought I'd lost it. I meant to give it to you sooner. I'm sorry."

She flipped on the wipers finally, wiped beneath her own eyes.

Underneath all the stamps, César's writing was just as I remembered it. And the thunder roared.

She dropped me off in front of school. I staggered in wet and heavy into the empty hallway. Opening the class door, they were watching I, CLAVDIVS again. Miss Cavazos jumped from her desk and led me back outside.

"What happened to the test?" I asked her.

"I postponed it till Monday."

"Really? Must have been some party last night."

"He didn't tell me. Your uncle, your mom, people just started showing up. I couldn't leave."

"Or didn't want to."

"This isn't about me," she said a bit more forcefully. "It's about Marcos. When did you last see him?"

"What's that got to do with anything?"

"Please, just tell me."

"Tell you what?" I said. "I'm not his mother. I hardly know him."

"But at the church. And Felix, he says you two—"

"Felix doesn't know shit," I shot back. "Just because we have the same last name, that doesn't mean I know him."

"You've never talked to me like that"

"Marcos does what he wants when he wants, okay? Just like you. Just like everybody else!"

She found her trophy behind the glass again. "He's gone," she said, her voice commanding, yet trembling.

"What?"

"Marcos is dead. My father told me this moring. I wanted you to know before I announce it to the class."

That stench enveloped me again. The janitor lady rolled out of the bathroom, this time waving an open palm.

Miss Cavazos came close. "I'm so sorry, Jaime. This news, and after what happened to your brother. Your mother mentioned it last night. I'm so sorry."

I pulled away and opened the classroom door. Up on the screen the Praetorian guards hacked Caligula down outside the vomitorium.

"And here he is again, everyone," announced Felix to the class, setting the laughter aflame. "CALI-CULO!!!"

I forearmed the lights. On the desk beneath the she-wolf, Romulus and Remus headbutted the same tit to mix the milk with blood. When I finally got to Felix, I aimed my knuckles at his eyes, Miss Cavazos screaming for help at the door.

Hey, Little Brother. Hope you're doing well.

I'm staying with the Professor and his sister, Marzia, in her house in Rome. She teaches at the university here, and every day after class she and I stop for espressos at her favorite café next to Trevi Fountain. We just got back from a tour of the Colosseum, finally. I couldn't get you that chunk I promised, but Marzia knows a little shop nearby where they make small replicas. I'll get you one soon, I promise. After helping the Professor with some of his research tomorrow he's promised to take me boar hunting in Umbria. It's a family tradition, Marzia says. I don't know why but I can't wait to see what she looks like holding a rifle in her hands.

And we won't just kill the beast, she tells me, we'll eat it too. If not, it's what's called "Crimine Di Caligola" in these parts. "Caligula's Curse." The legend is that Emperor Caligula was returning to Rome when two boars crossed his path. He grew so angry that he ordered his men to capture them, slice off their ears, disembowel them, and throw the guts and carcasses into the Tiber. He dedicated the slaughter to all the gods, but in his dreams they rebuked him. The next day Caligula was assassinated outside the Colosseum.

The meat's a rough chew, the Professor says, but good with the right wine. Especially the intestines, fried and mixed with pasta and garlic sauce. Marzia says that's her favorite too, but I don't know.

Anyways, there's no light in the patio right now and the sun is setting here and Marzia and the Professor want me in the pool with them. That's it for now, I guess. The one thing about Rome, Little Brother, is that the nights are longer here, so I find myself thinking a whole lot. If it's just you and Mom now, tell her I said hi. If Chato's still around, don't. I promise I'll write again before exams. I'll tell you what boar really tastes like.

Your bro,
César

Like nothing they'd ever seen, my uncle told Mom.

The way the fat man explained it to him, the police found no traces of anyone inside the trailer, the truck still out front. They followed the smell up the muddied drive to the shed where the dogs scrambled for the guts scattered all over the ground. They found Marcos with the rifle still in his mouth. The beast lay on its side, its belly enormous and ready to burst. It wasn't until they took hold of the hooves and tried dragging it out that Ernesto fell out in pieces, boots and all.

I hung under that crape myrtle again, fighting the obligation to enter the church, replaying those gruesome images in my head. I winced up at the new sign over the entrance where the fat man had chosen to go with the verse from Saint Peter, and I remembered hearing on Mom's Christian station the special way Peter died that day. How the Romans had captured him and sentenced him to death, just like his friend Jesus. How, feeling unworthy, he'd demanded they crucify him too but upside down. I pictured everything upside down beyond that door. "!hajullelaH" the congregation singing. The water pouring up not down from the back of Mom's head and back onto the small saucer. The fat man's ring around her finger, dissolving back through time and into the elements from which it had been forged.

I dropped my arms and walked away.

At the park the rain from the last few days had settled into puddles along the grass. The birds fluffed feathers, stole beakfuls, then flew away. The benches along the path sat damp and empty beneath the mesquites hoarding the stuffy air. I walked through the columns. The amphitheater was a pool of tense water, just like the Tiber César had written me about, centuries after the carcasses were heaved in by Caligula's centurions.

I sat down on the top step.

"Everyone's looking for you," Miss Cavazos said from behind me. And as she finally opened up about everything, I swear I saw Marcos and César rising from out of the dark water below, battle-scarred from helmet to sandal, arms extended in a Roman salute.

Miss Cavazos opened her palm when my hand found hers.

"After the rain," I said, "wuh-what comes next?"

She grunted to clear her throat.

"Hail," she said, and helped me back up.

UNITED IRRIGATION DISTRICT

They're building the Wall there, she said to him, and he couldn't even look at her.

He'd been there, you see, just off that bend in the highway, behind their home and down the side road where the twin port-a-potties guarded the entrance with one door proudly proclaiming

UID

NO TRESPASSING

VIOLATORS WILL BE PROSECUTED

He'd stormed out there late one day and kicked dirt beneath the dipping sun, stopping to watch as each hard-hatted, long-sleeved torso transformed into sun-slapped workers abandoning bulldozers and excavators and falling down that grand, flattened mountain of south Texas caliche, toting toolboxes and thermoses and, heaviest of all, the tired promise of going home, finally. They tossed their burdens into their truck beds, slapped palms, and mufflered away in different directions.

He waited for the last of the trucks to speed off, blaring to an old corrido that sang of kingpins and cartels, then finally crossed the road. He staggered up that loose dirt, a man on a mission, each step a chore, each step another argument, until he reached the top of the mound and peered into the biggest hole his eyes had ever seen.

They're building the Wall, I tell you.

He didn't respond, rolled the window down instead. He thought he caught an accordion somewhere, broad-chested laughter and mufflers, but the highway continued on in front of them, as empty as ever. And as the wind slapped his face, he couldn't help but think that maybe, just maybe, she was right.

ANAGRAM

We slouch side by side as she struggles to toothpick the tiny bits of meat jammed into the narrow at the tips of her incisors.

I can't—

Answer her, sister says.

And we throb there like choked kidneys, gasping into the viscous night.

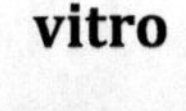

Dig

At Kamayakli the tunnel resembles a parched throat to Julio. It gapes long and deep before the front of the group in the lantern light. He palms the cool, carved limestone pressing round him to escape the thought of being swallowed. But it's no use; there it is: Temo, all those years ago, and the pulp he resembled when they finally pulled him out of the canal. Ever since then Julio's father had made it the Cortázar custom each time his son wandered off to say *I don't want to have to dig you out, too*, and as a boy he'd done his best to obey. The walkway narrows. The sides scrape the tips of his elbows and steal him from his memories.

A sharp elbow digs into his chest. *Keep up, Julio. We're almost there.* Lara's words bounce off the stone and back to where he staggers. He smiles in the dark knowing he trusts her.

The light widens; the air changes. Julio notices a pair of pudgy tourists coming into the light: a camera-strapped Frodo and Sam, he imagines playfully, joining him in this descent into Moria. They mumble hurriedly at each other in a language he doesn't understand. He laughs to himself while Lara muffles her own amusement in front of him. The rest of the group settles into their spines and shadows in the dancing pool of kerosene light.

...Doctor Lara Cortázar, the tour guide calls out.

And Julio watches his wife slice through the crowd and out under a wide and heavy archway. She begins in that raspy tone he loves and admires and everyone listens intently, even Frodo and Sam beside him. He half-smiles again as his wife goes on about the one central, cavernous well, and then the wide silos ten stories down, then the ancient stable they are standing in which she helped excavate, and, finally, how the entire complex served as an ancient stronghold against Arab invaders. Julio imagines that this is what Lara is saying, anyways, for her Turkish is as foreign to him as hard sunlight where he stands.

Shh, she demands, and like everyone else, Julio captures the music of trickling water, somewhere.

She resumes. Her words, her presence, they are ominous in that creviced light. Shadows slowly shift. The congregation bobs collective heads at everything Lara says. As if they'd all gladly calcify hundreds of feet below the surface of the earth, Julio included, just for the chance to hear more.

This; here. See, Julio?
Where, Lara? There?
Doesn't hurt, though.
It's big; right there. Right?
Ah! But don't! Don't squeeze it.
Okay; I won't. I promise; I won't.

Since Tenochtitlán, Julio's father instructs him from the edge, but as a boy he decides to shrug his shoulders. He doesn't care. Not this early in the morning. Not in this stench. Not on this day of all days! He pinches his nose with one set of fingers and with the other picks the crusty stuff from the sides of his eyes. The sun pokes through a thin slit between a pair of skyscrapers and blurs across the dark sewer water still sleeping in the long row of numbered pools.

Paunchy in his thick diving suit, Julio compares his father to an astronaut.

Nezahualcóyotl, Julio, the great poet and emperor of Tezcoco, he helped construct them, and the Mexica used these sewers before

Cortés arrived to pump the filth out, just like we do today. It's when things get stuck down there that I have to go in and clear it all out.

Julio's young stomach grumbles, and he remembers the chorizo sandwich his father had prepared for him back home, and the vow he'd secretly made not to take one bite from it, just to show his father who was boss.

Eh, mi topo? What do you think? Or are you still mad at me for getting you up so early?

Julio hates his nickname, but he endures it, like his hunger. Don Tacho arrives, his father's friend and co-worker, carrying a heavy helmet before of him, fastened to a pair of flaccid cables.

And now, time to go to work, mi topo. Happy Birthday!

The loud thrum from the oxygen compressor startles Julio. Before he can finally give in and confess his hunger to his father Don Tacho locks the helmet into place, and the boy watches his father tow the cables with him to the edge of the second pool, leap in feet first, and sink straight down.

Julio's stomach churns. On the concrete the cables palpitate like exposed veins.

I am sad, I grieve
I, lord Nezahualcóyotl.
With flowers and with songs
I remember the princes
Those who went away...

Temo stuffs the squib in the hole, lights it, nearly trips on the train track backing away. It sizzles there until POP!, forcing Julio to wince. He opens his young eyes to tiny bits of cindered newspaper fluttering down on dust as Temo lets out another celebratory guffaw, returns to the same spot, punches his fist into his right pocket for a second palomita, and uses his incisors to pull out the fuse a bit more. He bends down to give it flame, backs up next to Julio again.

POP!

¡Eso!, Temo celebrates.

In the summer heat the smell of gun powder nauseates Julio more than usual. He spots a cacique darting fast across the sky and into the arbor of a wide guamuchil nearby. Further on, deep in the east, he can see Popocatépetl and Iztaccíhuatl in tall sleep, their peaks tipped with spongy snow.

Vámonos, he finally says, fighting back the taste of sweat from his upper lip.

Just one more, Julio. To get them out.

We can do them by the canal, Temo. I told you: if my father sees me, I won't be able to go.

Uno mas, Julio. Just to get them out. Then we go.

Temo pulls a new squib out, a fat one, makes for the hole again. Frustrated, Julio leans in and curves a sandaled foot onto one of the old abandoned tracks. He looks behind him down the lazy street busy with a lone fruit vendor, seated on a stool by his cart and swatting flies.

POP!

Hah! What I tell you, cabrón? Eh, Julio? Look at them! Look!

The dust and newspaper particles begin to settle, and Julio can finally see the exiting horde. They crawl out of their hole in all directions and up and over one another, the fire ants, the same way he and Temo and the other boys spill out of the classroom each day, fondling any girls they can along the way. He jumps on the track so the ants don't get at his toes.

And they're mad as fuck, Julio. Ahora sí—¡Vámonos!

And they leap in tip toes, laughing, as they bound past the guamuchil leading to the path down to the canal.

Julio is brooding over the notes for his lecture on the sacrificial practices depicted in the Codex Magliabechiano, waiting for the words and images to synapse into solid thoughts within his throbbing skull, when a crisp page slices his thumb. He does not flinch. He holds up his finger to watch the red gather into a heavy glob that clings to his skin like a tiny, stubborn heart, unsure of when or where to fall.

A soft tap sounds on his office door.

"Julio? Are you in there? It's me. It's Eva."

He hides his hand beneath his desk as the door slowly opens.

"Oh. You *are* here. Hi. I…I just heard. I'm so sorry. Are you okay?"

He does not look at her. He gives her the same, tired response he's given everyone else.

"I'm so sorry," she says again, and he can tell by her tone that she is.

She closes the door, moves closer to his desk. She tells him, if he wants her to, she can come over tonight. Just to talk, of course. Nothing else. But he doesn't know how to answer her.

"All right. Okay," she says, and she is gone.

He sits there, wondering what the blood on his thumb has decided to do.

With hands handcuffed behind her the first of the Indian girls winks. *Papasito,* another one says, her mouth puckering between high cheekbones, blowing out a kiss. A third spreads her knees and rolls her hips slow.

Julio takes the last deep drag from his cigarette, flicks the butt on the asphalt, tugs at the neck on his heavy vest. The humid air delivers the gas fumes from the long lines of semis and SUVs trailing from the checkpoint booths. Next to the women the off-duty dogs lie motionless in their cages, each turned flaccid, furry lumps by the south Texas heat.

Looking good, Professor! ¡Chingón! You ready? Shit, man. Still can't believe you showed, Cousin.

Pedro's voice is loud; his handshake, hot leather. His Oakleys reflect Julio, but stretched.

Had to get out, Julio responds.

I hear you, man. How is Lara these days? Better, I hope?

The women blow high-pitched air through their teeth to get Julio's attention. They lick their chapped lips. The oldest and pudgiest punches her tongue into her cheek, over and over.

Something, eh? Pedro says. *They do that, Primo. The coyotes tell them to. It's so we'll let them go. But it's bad news for these. Watch. Muchachas,* and Pedro uses his Tex-Mex Spanish to explain to the women that Julio doesn't matter. That he's insignificant. Not a real agent, even. A waste of their breaths and lures and hips.

The women hang their conquered heads.

Hah, Pedro celebrates. *Works every time. We're out in a bit, Primo. Hang tight. They won't bother you no more.*

Cool air snares Pedro through the station doors.

And Julio quickly realizes the women have forgotten all about him, won't look at him, won't hope for him anymore. He feels the depth of his betrayal like the thumps from his heart beneath the sweat on his skin. The women break into a powerful song in their native tongue, forcing the dogs from their siestas, but too lazy still to curve up into their spines and dance.

The doorbell rings louder than usual. Julio rises from his recliner and staggers to the front door. He peeps through the hole to catch a glimpse. *What do you see?* he imagines someone asking him from behind, just as they'd asked Howard Carter at the foot of Tutankhamen's tomb.

Wonderful things, Carter had answered back.

Wonderful things.

At the Wall the Jews pray. Julio can make out the rambling figures through the rental's bug-battered battlefield of a windshield. Hundreds of the faithful shifting and gathering all along the base of the ancient stone structure, bobbing their heads and torsos. He scales the height of the Wall with his heavy eyes, up to where the Jerusalem sky unfurls. To where the sun bristles wide on Mohammed's golden dome. Where the lean minaret in the distance spears into nothing but an expanse of blue behind it.

He parks behind a row of minivan taxis hugging the curb, and just like that, Lara is gone. He doesn't try to stop her. He climbs out of the rental car instead, leans against the Enterprise logo, lights a Marlboro, and watches as Lara cuts through the crowd and disappears. He buys a Coke from a passing vendor and takes a long swig while a group of olive-skinned drivers ogle him suspiciously. They erupt into broken English all around him, offering their cabs to all passersby they take for Americans.

That morning back home. Julio remembers waking up to relieve himself, only to find Lara curled around the toilet once more, the water in the white porcelain turned a pink mess. He remembers bathing her, helping her back to bed, and calling in to cancel their respective classes for the next couple of days. Then the idea that surfaced from her own sore throat. *Just in case*, she'd said, squeezing his hand, and he'd agreed. He'd purchased the tickets right after she'd fallen asleep again, fumbling through the credit card numbers with the agent on the phone due to a nagging tremble in his lower jaw, until he finally got the digits out right.

No!, he repeats, forcefully this time, so that the yarmulked man stops pointing at Julio's rental, stops insisting in a language Julio doesn't understand, and continues on his way. The taxi drivers snicker and enjoy the justice done. Julio finally finds Lara in the distance. Sticking the last of his cigarette in the Coke bottle, he sees his wife at the foot of the eastern part of the Wall. He watches her fold her piece of paper once, twice, three times, and stuff it into a crevice between two massive stones.

Then a voice descends from the sky in wonderful trills, a voice that Julio doesn't comprehend but that compels him, drowning in its power the roar of the traffic behind him. Lara is immovable in the distance. The Coke vendor reappears. He shrugs off a group of thirsty tourists, then falls to his knees to pray.

and as the crane comes down on this day of all days julio pretends his father is landing with life on the earth for the first time and that his own young tears are due to the pangs from his hungry hunger and not his fathers descent into the world where Julio now watches him drip down drip down drip down down

...zan nihualayocoya, nicnotlamati.
ayoquic, ayoc,
quenmanian,
titechyaitaquiuh in tlalticpac
yca, nontiya, yehua, ohuaya, ohuaya...

"Hi," but Eva says this timidly at the door, without lifting her eyes, unsure almost, as if preparing to hear something harsh before being sent away. But Julio doesn't do that. He moves to the side and lets her in. He studies Eva's careful amble to the love seat where she drops her lump of a purse, and just like that it begins. She is apologizing again, offering her condolences again, while the diamonded, decorative skull on the side of her purse glowers at him, so that he has no choice but to give in. So that he's thrust back into those pits in Perú with Lara all over again, where once the hard dirt sprouted nothing but tiny skulls.

Fresh ones, Primo! Hah! Not like you're used to, eh, Julio?
Cut at the wrists and stacked one over the other, the hands lie at the tunnel's entrance; a man's hands with girthy fingers.

Pedro chuckles and pokes a playful elbow into the back of Julio's bulletproof vest, assuring him he is not dreaming. The gun-drawn agents hurry past Julio, climbing one after the other into the hole in the broken concrete, until their clatter leaves the echoes of the warehouse to themselves.

You picked a hell of a day for your ride-a-long, Julio, tell you that much. We don't see this setup that often. The hands, I mean. This

*is special, Primo. Ceremonial, even. Right up your alley, Cousin.
Watch.*

And Julio can't stop his own hands, his jaw from trembling.
Somewhere in the expanse of the warehouse, the dogs bark and
echo in frenzy, while all around him the tall stacks of cellophaned
boxes marked "EE.UU." seem ready to crash down on him like
some ancient, collapsing portico, determined to bury him where
he stands. He thinks of Lara at that instant. Of Eva. The women
at the station, too. Their veiled, majestic verses fading as the bus
took them all away.

Pedro answers a static voice on his two-way radio in low mumbles. He unsheathes his collapsible baton and pries it under the
bloated hands, flopping them over slowly.

Crazy things..., he says.

Beneath the congealed red there is a photograph of a man and
woman, lost in their smiles.

And what did the doctor say?
Nothing.
Nothing?
Just stress.
Slow down then, Lara.
I will, Julio. I promise. Now, read to me some more...

...o ayc ompolihuiz in moteyo...
anca za ye in cocuic a yca
nihualchoca,
yn zan nihualicnotlamatico,
nontiya, ehua, ohuaya, ohuaya...

He leads Lara away from the votive jade saucers he knows
so well, leads her past the clumps of tourists gawking over the
display of ceremonial masks, through the rope cordoning off the
entrance to the small causeway flanked by the chac-mools. He

points at the wide, circular monolith encompassing the breadth of the wall as hidden speakers pulse into his ears with the sounds of palmed drums. For a split second he is tugged on by time, so that he can't help but imagine the scent of sweet copal pluming from a saucerful of beating hearts. His own organ beats fast. Fast enough to make him hard.

Who...what is this, Lara asks, mesmerized.

He presses into her, forcing a blush. He clears his throat and his head and explains that the scattered limbs and torso depicted on the massive stone relief belong to Coyolxauhqui, the Mexica Moon goddess, dismembered by her brother the War God for rebelling against him.

She bites his shoulder.

Julio, Lara whispers, *you will never vanquish me.*

> *...we're to pass away. I say, "Be pleasured!"—*
> *I that am Nezahualcóyotl.*
> *Ah, do we truly live on earth...*

The seed pods are on tight and chafe loud around Julio's young knees and forearms as he cuts through the thick crowd with his father in the lead. The kaleidoscope feathers from his father's head-dress rainbow out and brush over bowed heads in slow procession towards the Basilica doors. The air reeks of gun powder, sweet chamomile from Xochimilco, and meats and maize fried in lard. Beyond the tricolored flags and ceremonial banners, he catches a glimpse of the long row of penitents, dragging their bellies across the Zócalo's cold stone on their hands and knees.

His father stops suddenly. Julio rattles to a halt behind him. The jaguar set into the back of his father's vest is an intricate inlay made up of polished jade from Iztapalapa and precious shells from Tehuantepec. Embarrassed to look up, he feels the tugs on his own set of quetzal feathers. He fidgets from the probing fingers starting to explore other parts of his costume. Once his father is off again, Julio is relieved. Hot wax from a votive candle finds his left shoulder, but he endures the pain. The evening chill crashes against his skin. Balms over his flesh to ease the burn.

Julio! Julito! Over here! Don Tacho's voice is powerful enough to reach them above the sounds of the crowd. He waves at them from the foot of the Old Basilica's western spire, his own thick plumage radiating from his head. The old man sits back down by the other musicians and dancers, lays the log drum across his lap, and tightens the leather straps on both sides. He tests his handiwork with a few hollow thumps. The sound reaches Julio and seems to delve into the nexus of noise all around him, jabbing at it, forcing it to listen.

Today is the day, eh, Julito? Are you ready? Don Tacho's calloused hands leave his drum for the sagging pods around Julio's knees. *These have to be on tight, Julito. The last thing you want is for these to fall off while you dance. You're Tlayeconqui, you're Dance Leader, today. You need to shine! Shine for the Virgen, Julito! For México!*

As Don Tacho tightens, Julio's father approaches his son and hands him a wide, feathered shield and a sword studded with blunted chips of obsidian.

Your chimalli. Your macquahuitl. You'll be fine, mi topo. Just like we practiced. Let's go. It's time.

And Julio watches as the other dancers rise to take their places. His knees tremble, rattle all the way up to the front of the square. He focuses on his breathing, just as his father told him to do to beat off any nerves. He notices the red-green-white streamers and the confetti in flight, fluttering down slowly, only to get trampled. A man, woman, and child pick their spot, nonchalant in their matching Paul VI t-shirts. From nearby Puebla, Julio surmises, a group of Chichimeca women huddle over their children in their traditional china poblana outfits, each wrapped in bobbled shawls, their wide castor skirts hovering over wet brown feet in leather huaraches. And above all are the banners of the Indian, Juan Diego

Cuauhtlatoatzin, with the image of Guadalupe, the Mother of God, of México, seared into the threads of his mantle.

He hears the drums.

He begins.

> and don tacho wont let him grabs him blocks him from the torn mass of vulcanized rubber on the concrete edge that is the still torso of his father as the workers scramble and the shrill sirens puncture this day of all days this day of all days this day of all days

And it's Julio as careful as always, still sitting Indian-style in his assigned spot and relying on his steady wrist to brush over that nub of hard earth, careful not to damage the treasures below. But every now and then when no one is looking it's him giving in to the urge and flicking a little harder, so that the grains can reach the skin on the back of Lara's young hand. *Sorry,* he finally says, not meaning it, of course, looking straight at her, watching her stick out her tongue and a dusty middle finger. He's answering back with a wink as the sounds of the pounding mattocks come muffled just over the surrounding dunes.

That evening it's him even more wary. He's eating dinner with the other exchange students but speaking sparsely, only qualifying statements here and there so as not to stand out. No one mentions anything, and he is glad, just as Lara gropes his thigh beneath the table and forks another piece of pork from the estofado on her plate.

Later that night, it's him waiting for the tents to go out. He is heading with Lara for the edge of the excavation site where the cool ocean breeze makes it difficult to light their cigarettes, but they manage. She is lying on his lap blowing rings while he recites his favorite of Nezahualcóyotl's poems again, and he is laughing as she tries to pronounce the more complicated words. She punches him on his shoulder playfully. He leans forward to warm his lips on hers.

Thanks, he says.

For?

Not mentioning it.

Oops, Lara says.

He hears them singing at the top of their lungs first before turning to see a wide shadow coming straight towards him. A giggling mass shuffling clumsily through the sand, guarding a single flicker of light at its center.

Happy twenty-fifth! Lara is saying, pressing her lips to his cold cheek.

And he is hating that he wants her.

And they are all pounding his shoulders and squeezing his ass and handing him Pilsen beers that will freeze in his fist if he nurses them too long, so he chugs them down fast. He tells them he doesn't like frosting, so they eat the cake themselves. The lights from Trujillo begin to pulse from far away. They urge him to close his eyes for his present. He does. And it's Julio in his own dark, spinning, picking out Lara's laugh from among all the rest.

Julio brings his book and Lara's ankh amulet, the one he once purchased for her at the foot of Khufu's pyramid that summer day, where the old Bedouin leaned across the table and claimed to have led the newlywed Crowleys into the King's Chamber in 1904. Julio had wanted to hear the whole story, of course—about Alistair and Rose, about grimoires and black rituals—but the old Bedouin would say no more. So Julio had picked the amulet out from all the other trinkets on the table, brushed the sand and thick auburn hair from Lara's strong shoulders, and clasped the chain at the base of the back of her neck.

Julio? Is that you?

But now.

Yes, Lara. It's me.

He bends over her, kisses her cold forehead. She offers a frail smile. She motions feebly with her right hand, and Julio understands. He carefully lifts her hairless head and brings the chips of ice to her lips to quench her thirst. He listens to her molars, muffled beneath the pruney flesh of her lips, crunching on the ice. On the nightstand next to her the lilies spill petals over the get-well cards.

And work? Do they miss me much, Julio?

They do.

Has Eva finished indexing my notes?

I haven't seen her.

He flicks off the television, sits in the chair beside her bed. He opens his book to his favorite of Nezahualcóyotl's poems.

I'll try not to fall asleep this time, Julio, I promise. Not like last night. I'll try. Real hard this time.

He believes her, his hands quaking softly beneath the book's spine.

> *...not forever on earth, but briefly here.*
> *Even jades are shattered.*
> *Gold, broken.*
> *Ah! Plumes, splintered.*
> *Not forever on earth, but briefly here...*

And it's the mattocks in Julio's head now, trying to pick their way out, and his body—heavy, thirsty, stretched. He is washing the sand from his face and hair as best as possible, hardly remembering the previous night, struggling into his overalls, unsure of the time of day except for the bright parallelogram at the foot of his tent's entrance. He is listening to the shuffle of hurried feet and excited voices outside as he reaches for his sun hat before heading out.

Bodies are blurring past him, scurrying towards the main mound where the locals are resting their chins on pickaxes and peering down into the excavation area that Julio knows so well. Amidst the din he can hear the ocean, the morning swells as eager as ever to carry off a little more sand.

And it's him scampering down the well-worn path to the start of the cordoned grid, ignoring the taste of alcohol rising from the back of his throat, spitting it all out. And he is finding Lara on her knees in his usual spot, with the main archaeologist hovering over her shoulder anxiously, urging a giddy Lara to brush ever so gently over the row of child-sized skulls.

"And...how was Lara, Julio?"

"What?"

"As good; better?"

"What does that matter?"

"I'm sorry; forget I asked."

"The things you say."

"Just come; here."

and the sounds are of rain going up then down and in and out and to the side and julios plumage wisping through the cool air on one foot turning on the other the same the other way the cold stone slapping his soles like the eyes around him shield up then down sword thrust bring it back its a dance a dance that he knows because his father taught him the steps over and over like the mexica the aztecs like they danced before the tzompantli the skull rack where the captured warriors lost precious ventricled organs he is careful as if dancing between rain drops comfortable with his body his limbs lost in the chilly night he decides to close his eyes his next step is confident but the ground is not he brings his knees up to his chest stabs into the air his soles descend like falcons in the dive and wedge between the manhole

cover and the rims outside edge don tacho loses his
rhythm a collective gasp he feels the warm breaths
before him behind him as he plummets in in
feathered glory he pretends its not him but the world
that is falling away until after the crack of his bones
he endures the pain and suffers the voices above him
mi topo where are you julito are you all right but he
won't answer not yet not yet not yet

Julio quits reading. He focuses instead on the thin chain trailing down Lara's arm, the amulet cupped in fragile hands crossed solemnly on her chest.

He closes his book. Before pulling the blanket up to Lara's chin, he can't help but surrender to the geography of her bones: toes to wasting knees to her wan neck. His glance falls on the valley of Lara's face, her cheekbones jutting out at him like two pallid Hissarlik temples, crumbling in a slow-motion storm.

And Julio realizes he is no warlock about to exercise great power over life and death.

No hawk-headed Horus or Beast 666.

No Aztec god or vengeful brother.

That all he can do is be present.

Exist as she fades.

and as he dresses to race home julio is jealous so
jealous of temos somersaults from the concrete edge
and of the way the water delivers his friend each time
and drips from the hair and heavy flesh between his
legs so that julio endures the sear of his young soles
on the hot concrete on purpose and watches one final
time as temo jumps gloriously up and out of his
memory and into the sun and water again

And they finally rouse him. The buried ones. With drums.

Julio envisions them, forming and gathering into their bodies, their essences curling out from his memories like sacred plumes from saucered incense. Clawing their way up to him from under some ancient, gargantuan stone.

He rustles from under Eva's arm, out of bed, and rushes out the bedroom door.

"Julio, wait. Where are you going?"

He knows the hole he digs will be bottomless.

THE RUNNER

And Susana persisted that evening until he pushed her hand away and jumped out of bed. He slalomed past Susana's textbook and highlighters on the floor, past his little Jenny sound asleep in her crib, past that low Tonight Show laughter converging with Susana's platitudes—"Felix, it's okay. It happens."—and bolted out the bedroom door. He stumbled into the bathroom, closed and locked the door to leave it all behind. "Come on, Feli. Open up. I told you. It's all right." He flushed the toilet to drown her out. "Whatever," she finally said. He pulled down his boxers and sat on the toilet, the weight of his chin digging his elbows into his knees.

He finished and tossed the tissue into the small wastebasket sitting next to his little Jenny's potty. He rose with a sigh, pulled up his boxers. He reached to flush again when he noticed the first kernel, then a second, a third one, more. A slew of them bobbing stubbornly within the froth and mass of his mess. And he teetered there in the realization that his insides lacked the conviction to break the corn down.

"On your left!" the man blared behind Felix, so that he surrendered to his bones and staggered to the right of the asphalt path to let the man pass. He caught the poodle first—its crabby snout; its neck stuffed through a black collar; its tail tipped with frizz like the tall weeds decorating his front lawn. Felix followed the taut leash and found it fastened to a pale, freckled hand where a wrist watch blinked at him with morning sun.

And like that Felix prepared to catch sight of the man who had shouted. But *had* he shouted? He thought of Susana there, panting in that break in his run, and how she liked to accuse him of being awfully judgmental at times. A character flaw that, according to her, was no doubt due to the Mexican in him. "Dick found it somewhere online during class," she explained that one night, sliding her biology textbook and highlighters across his chest, letting them fall, then toeing into his toes. "It's all minorities. We all carry this anger. Since colonization." He remembered laughing at first, then doing his very best to fixate on the soft allure of her palm brushing past his navel.

But nothing.

"So angry," she whispered, hot in his ear, "when all we need do is relax. Forget. Let go. Get used to those who like to be on top."

A bead of sweat trailed into the corner of Felix's left eye, launching him back into the present, just as the man who had shouted came into view. The old man sauntered bright-skinned into Felix's view as if the whole of the asphalt path had long ago been cleared of beasts and savages just for him. He passed Felix without so much as a nod, a quick glance, not even a pop of a pair of fingers. Felix curled over to check on his laces, pulled the knots tight. By the time he looked up again the man who had shouted was off the path and headed for a yellow Fiat parked on the grass along the drowsy highway.

The Fiat mufflered away and Felix started on his run again. As he trotted, he felt compelled to will himself into a pair of clenched fists, a rolling of both his shoulders, one-two-three deep breaths, all to assure himself that he still commanded his own body. He did this while replaying that moment when his bones had shifted their weight inside him (*On your left!*), urging his thirty-year old body to the right and out of the way. He sped up, pondering brains and bones, synapses and sinews, all concepts he'd gleaned from Susana's textbook, and how and why these all worked—or failed?—collectively to move him out of the way. He heard Susana (*Whatever...*), ran even faster, slid a sweaty palm through his thinning hair. He focused on the cumulus clouds in that expanse of south Texas sky and the sun on stilts inside it. He bolted past a Frito's bag hooked into the brush along the path, its cellophane seared white from the strain of too much sun.

The healthy dinner Susana prepared that evening consisted of a cup's worth of brown rice, a George Foreman-grilled beef liver steak with sautéed onions, and another cup of those sweet corn kernels straight out of a Green Giant microwavable bag. For his little Jenny in her high chair next to him, a plastic Mickey Mouse bowl filled to the brim with those steaming kernels. He poured ice water into his mug and watched his little Jenny fist bunches of kernels into her mouth.

"You know how you get, Feli," said Susana, slicing her liver into bite-sized squares in front of him. "I bet he was just being polite. At Dollar General, I get yelled at too, by all sorts of people. But you can't get mad. Dick taught me that. He taught me to tell myself it's just the world we live in and that's just the way people are." She sipped from her ice water. "I'm sure the man just didn't want you bumping into him or his dog. That's all. You know how you get, Feli."

By the end of Susana's exegesis, the ice in Felix's mouth numbed his tongue. His eyes had wandered from his little Jenny too and set themselves to boring a hole into the food in front of him. The liver and kernels steamed up and onto his face, through his nostrils, throbbed in the back of his throat with the taste of anticipation. But Felix could not eat. He nibbled on the sides of his tongue instead and pondered the possibility that, just as his wife surmised, the man who had shouted (*On your left!*) might actually have been looking out for him all along. Perhaps the man who had shouted (*On your left!*) had done so only to avoid an unpleasant scene between Felix's calves and that ferocious poodle of his. Felix imagined it clearly—that wolf-worthy scowl curled deep into that snout, ready and willing to bite a chunk out of him unless he cleared out of the way and fast. His stomach growled with that poodle's menacing snarl from behind those blaring fangs, long and sharp, inching ever closer for a taste of Felix's flesh.

"Dick gave me Thursday off for your follow-up," Susana continued, "and we don't have class, either. We'll pay with the cash we usually use for Bita. You told her we won't need her Thursday, right?"

But inside Felix's mind that ultimatum continued to sound, a crack of a whip of words, booming between his ears even louder than when it first commanded him.

"Can't we hire someone else, Feli? That old lady doesn't listen."
(*On your left!*)
"You don't like your dinner?"
(*On your left!*)
"When Jenny finishes, you take her to see if she potties, okay?"
(*On your left!*)
"Have you talked to Jesse yet?"
(*On your left! On your left! On your left!*)
"Felix?!"

And Felix's body remembered. He shifted to get out of the way again, elbowed his little Jenny's chair, and sent her bowl of kernels crashing to the floor.

He heard the fork fall first, then the hard clink from the knife. Wails from his little Jenny. Susana pulling her from the high chair, scurrying away, the bedroom door going *SLAM!* With the last of the day's light oblonging in, Felix studied the diaspora of kernels on the kitchen floor. And he trembled in his chair thinking how foolish it would be to give in a third time. To spring out of his chair in obeisance and trounce on those kernels without remorse.

The following morning Felix left the apartment earlier than usual. He rose from the couch, slipped into shorts and a t-shirt in that living room dark, laced his Nikes tight, washed his face and brushed his teeth in the kitchen sink, all to be gone before Susana awoke for work. Before the neighbor, Bita, arrived to care for his little Jenny. He kissed two fingers and pressed them gently onto the Sears photograph of his daughter on the mantle. He grabbed his keys and locked the door as quietly as possible.

Outside on the small porch Felix spread his legs wide and bent over to stretch. He counted to thirty in cadence with the early-morning crickets, the sultry south Texas air slowly filling his lungs. He straightened up, brought both feet together, bent over to stretch some more, up again, then two, three deep breaths, in through the nose, out the mouth. He started on his usual trot towards Military Highway, the sun just starting to yawn and stretch itself up and over the rooftops on his right.

He jogged past the dew-tipped weeds adorning his lawn, past the stink from his trash can, the Sanchez's, the Treviño's, the Benitez's, all of them slouching along the curb, drowsy and dewy themselves. He peered over Bita's trash can and into her hedge of ixoras where a neighborhood cat sat still as a statue and stared at him wide-eyed. He made out the old woman's doughy silhouette on her porch finally, her silver hair just starting to glow through the waning morning shadows. The rest of her sat hunched on a chair, shelling a piece of corn between her palms effortlessly, loosening kernels that fell one after the other into a bucket at her feet.

And it was at that moment—just as Susana's mandate rang in his ears and he prepared to stop and tell Bita about his doctor's appointment the following day—that Felix realized he was witnessing the origins of those corn tortillas the old woman liked to bring over daily. Those warm tortillas he and his little Jenny enjoyed so much—the inside smothered in butter, then rolled up. Those same tortillas Susana tossed into the trash when she found them after coming home from work or school. "That woman!" she'd fume each time, until finally one day, "I've told her over and over, Felix. Now you're going to tell her—*no more tortillas!* Jenny shouldn't be eating this, you either. Don't you remember what the doctor said?" *Okay, okay*, he'd said to placate her, trying his best to recall Dr. Carr's decree against Bita's corn tortillas. He could not forget that evening a few months back, though—the steamed Brussel sprouts and chicken breast lying bland and tasteless on the plate in front of him; Susana ripping into the Green Giant microwavable bag for the first time; his little Jenny gobbling up those kernels; then that phone call from Jesse with the news that the company was going through a rough patch, and that letting him go was supposed to make things better. He'd forgotten all about chastising Bita after, that, gladly accepting each new batch of tortillas, but making sure to toss them in the trash can outside before Susana came back home.

He was picturing that buttery smirk on his little Jenny's face when Bita finally spoke.

"Buenos dias, Felix."

"Buenos dias."

He returned from the thought of his little Jenny to notice he'd stopped running. His right foot seesawed on the curb; his right elbow rested atop Bita's trash can. He could still hear the crickets too, the last of them serenading the sun riding warmer atop his head and shoulders. He peered up at the old woman, still hard at work on that corn. Then Felix let it all out as if he were the one being shelled, tossing the kernels of his feeble Spanish into the old woman's ears.

"Bita. Mañana, no. Doctor, yo."

Bita said nothing. She went on shelling that corn between her palms, one thick-wristed hand over the other, in swift semicircles, back and forth, the taps from those bucket-bound kernels reminding Felix of his little Jenny's soles slapping playfully on his chest.

A loud *boom!* in the distance silenced the remaining crickets and sent that cat darting deeper into rustling Ixoras. Bita loosened the last of the kernels, then dropped the naked cob to her right. She produced a new girthy specimen from her lap, waved it at Felix.

"Okay," she said.

Felix prepared to wave back, but not before a familiar warmth began to invade his groin. He looked down, up at Bita, down again at the growing bulge, with that cat on his scalp-turned-scratching post, the flesh of his face on fire. He moved behind the trash can for cover, snapped a hand into the front of his shorts, then out again. The trash truck screeched around the corner, its headlights searching for Felix, leaving him nowhere to hide. He ran away savagely, with Bita still waving, scratching his scalp furiously, his pulsing glans not going away.

"My God, Felix," Susana said into the sun visor, flipped it back up. "You and your ideas."

His ideas! He pushed the gearshift into P and sat there in protest, waiting for Susana to get out of the car. She exited finally, opened the rear door, freed his little Jenny from her car seat, and disappeared through Whataburger's double doors.

His ideas! He stepped out of the car finally, the midday traffic dopplering all around him, the sun bearing down hard. He pressed the lock on his keychain, made for the entrance, and wondered how on earth Susana could have missed it. She'd sat next to him in that quiet lobby, after all, still silent even after his apology for the kernel-toppling affair a few nights back, just as his little Jenny teetered down the row of chairs to that old woman's knobby knees. "Hello, princess," the woman said with a nervous jolt, then rushed to pull her red-scaled purse from his little Jenny's curious fingers. His daughter returned to a red-faced Susana, nibbling on the corner of a Cialis brochure she'd picked up along the way. The woman half-smiled, then flipped her purse open, snaked a hand in, pulled out a small vial of Purell, and lathered her palms, the arches between her fingers, even her knees. "So sorry," Susana repeated, over and over, her flush slowly fading, until the nurse opened the door and called Felix's name.

His ideas. Inside Whataburger, the rush of cool air soothed the sweat on Felix's lower back. The lunch rush about to start, the tables and fake pothoses waited for those midday rumps, food-filled trays, ketchup stains, and curious fingers. He recognized Garth Brooks on the speakers as his little Jenny ran into his knees with a giggle. He picked her up, nuzzled his nose into the arch of her left ear. Through her hair he watched Susana at the front counter, peering up at the menu over the shoulders of an elderly white couple.

And his desires! He recalled Dr. Carr's advice (*Remember: to get it up, you gotta give it up!*), but not before his salivary glands surrendered to the sizzle from the French fries, chicken strips, and onion rings, all of them bobbing in thick, boiling oil beside rows of half-pound beef patties searing majestically on windowpane-sized grills behind pimply teenagers in ball caps, orange polos, and black khakis. His little Jenny flicked the tip of her shoe into his groin. He held his breath, waited for the pain, and his eyes fell upon the salads piled high in a glass-paned refrigerator behind the front counter, soundless and boring in their clear, plastic containers.

"You go on first, honey," the woman before Susana drawled. "You got our permission, sweetheart. We're still thinking 'bout what we want."

"Really? Thank you so much," replied Susana. She turned to find Felix. "Thousand Island, right?"

The couple unpeeled their shoulders to let Susana through. Yoakam followed Brooks through the speakers, and it was as if the man who had shouted and the woman who had lathered dragged their instruments through Felix's nervous system and headed straight for the honky-tonk gathering in his brain. He turned from Susana in disgust, found a high chair for his little Jenny, lugged it to the nearest empty table. He strapped his little Jenny in and plopped himself down. And as more families poured in and rushed by in blurs Felix fumed as the old couple exercised their lips behind Susana, sly smiles on their faces, all in celebration of the sick gift of generosity they'd just imparted.

Susana arrived at the table a few moments later and sat beside his little Jenny. Without looking at Felix she set down two water bottles next to a tiny plastic tent with the number 69 on it. She reached into the diaper bag and brought out a disposable plate and a small Ziploc of corn kernels. She dumped the kernels onto the plate carefully. His little Jenny flailed her arms in anticipation, a sight that threatened to soothe the rumpus in Felix's head.

"She loves those kernels," he heard his mouth utter.

Susana twisted the cap off her water bottle, took a sip. "Yeah," she sighed.

"Yeah."

"Yes, Felix."

"Yeah," he repeated, and then he went for it: "I can't help what I see, Susana, okay? What *you* don't see."

"See what, Felix?" She twisted the cap back on tightly. "You're still with that woman at the doctor's office? Or what now? This nice couple that let me order our *fucking* salads?" She looked to the right, to the left, unsure if anyone heard her, then straight at Felix. "What's the matter with you? You worry about stuff like that, like this, when you should—"

"What?"

"Forget it."

"What should I worry about, Susana?"

"I said forget it."

He imploded into his ultimatum when he noticed her eyes had left him for the order number on the table. The music played on, and he imagined the band behind Yoakam—the couple at the counter on steel guitar and fiddle, Bita on drums, Jesse on a mean bass, Susana on background vocals, all of them producing the sexy song in his ears. And prostrate on the sawdust-covered floor of his neurons, the man who had shouted and the woman who had lathered, one inverted on top of the other, face to crotch, doing their thing.

"I meant Jesse," Susana said.

A young man in an orange polo, his face a pimpled mess, darted by with a trayful of neatly-wrapped burgers and fries. Susana reached over and flicked a stubborn kernel off his little Jenny's chin.

"I can't ask him," Felix said. "Not yet."

Susana shook her head, rolled her eyes. She dumped the rest of the kernels onto his little Jenny's plate.

"Lord have mercy! This little princess sure likes her corn, don't she?"

Looking up, Felix found the woman from the counter, patting the top of his little Jenny's head, a thick set of glasses magnifying marbly green eyes beneath white, popcorn hair.

"She does, yes," Susana answered, a polite smile on her face, then a nervous chuckle. "Thank you so very much."

"For what, darlin'?"

"Sorry?" asked Susana.

"What are you thankin' me for?"

"For your..."

"Yes?"

"...your compliment."

"Say again, dear?"

"You complimented my, our daughter."

"Uh-huh.

"Yes."

"And you thanked me. For what, sugar?"

Susana turned to Felix, back to the woman. "I'm sorry, I, uh..."

"Oh, I'm just teasin', hon," the woman cackled. "I know why. Sure. And you're very welcome, sweetheart." She patted Susana's head next. "Now, Jim," she continued, elbowing a tubby septuagenarian in a South Padre Island tank top behind her, tufts of white hairs on his shoulders, holding a pair of Styrofoam cups in one hand, their order number in the other. "You go on now. Do the same as I done," she commanded him. "You touch this sweet lil' princess. That's the custom down here. You remember what that Indian woman told us at the flea market, don't ya? We can't just look at people down here. Not like back home, no. We're foreigners, not from here, so we need to touch 'em all, or else. 'Evil something,' she called it. I don't remember."

"Evil Eye," Susana offered with a schoolgirl's urgency. "Yes, Ma'am. We believe that down here."

"Evil Eye! Yes! That's it! What a wonderful, lovely lil' superstition!" The woman's hand snaked down onto Susana's shoulder. The man behind her raked his bow across his fiddle, stared Felix down. "Exactly why we love comin' down here. Ain't that right, Jim? To mingle with folks like you, real folks. You and all your adorable lil' superstitions. Just wonderful. Ain't that right, Jim?"

"Yup," the man grunted. The woman came off Susana's shoulder and took the cups from her partner. Still staring Felix down, the man reached over and palmed his little Jenny's head.

A new song hovered down, a Strait shanty Felix recognized but could not place, just as that young man in the orange polo broke through the line at the front counter and arrived with two salads on a tray.

"Sixty-nine?" he asked.

"Yes," Susana said. "Felix?" With everyone looking at him, Felix picked up the number from the table and surrendered it over. The young man slid the tray onto the table.

"And what's our number, Jim?" the woman asked.

"One," her partner responded, showing her the tiny plastic tent.

"Yes, we are!" the woman proclaimed, palming both of Susana's shoulders this time, leaning in with all of the weight of her steel guitar.

"Yes, ma'am," Susana said awkwardly.

The woman straightened up, let Susana go. "Well, Jim, looks like it's time to let our new friends here eat."

"Thank you so very much," replied Susana.

"For what, darlin'?"

"I'm sorry. Did I—"

"Just teasin' you again, sweetie!" The woman swapped an invisible fly in front of Susana's face. "Y'all go on now. We'll let you eat. We'll let you enjoy your meal. Your healthy meal. Mmm. And bye, bye, princess!" She palmed his little Jenny once more, then hooked her partner's arm and led him away.

His little Jenny slapped her wet palms on the table playfully. Beyond the center tables, past a mother on her cellphone and her two boys stuffing French fries in their nostrils, at the tail-end of that Strait song, he heard that old woman's cackle again. Susana lifted the clear lid off her salad and poured Thousand Island over sliced grilled chicken, cherry tomatoes, a bed of lettuce squares.

"What?" she snapped at Felix.

He didn't say a word. He was reaching for his salad when his cellphone rang.

Felix stepped into Home Depot the following morning, his calves still sore following his usual run. He made it past the shopping carts and neatly-stacked, two-for-one Scotts Weed and Feed and Bug-B-Gone specials, and it wasn't long before he popped palms with some of his former co-workers. Manny from Plumbing quickly mentioned how thin he looked. "Pues, of course," said Zeke from Electrical. "Not working, so he's had all this time to—" and he finished by pumping his pelvis back and forth. The two men laughed, slapped Felix on the back. He told them about his meeting with Jesse and they made him promise to look for them afterwards for some more of their torture. He left them there arguing over which one of them would cover for someone named Mister Johnson.

Felix cut straight through Power Tools, past a browsing couple at the washer-dryer combos, all the way in past the porcelain toilets and replacement flush and fill valves. He reached the back of the store and stopped for a sip at the water fountain between the public restrooms. He made the turn into the employee lounge and took a deep breath before knocking on Jesse's half-open door.

"Come in."

Felix walked into Jesse's office and found him seated behind a wide, paper-filled desk, his dress shirt a pristine yellow, staring into a computer screen in front of him.

"Hey," he said without leaving the screen.

"Hey," Felix responded.

Jesse turned and reached into a mini-fridge behind him and pulled out a girthy black bottle that fit snuggly in his hand.

"Picked me up some Tejuino in Progreso last weekend," Jesse proclaimed. A two-gulp swig, then he twisted the lid back on. "You still hate it?"

"Yeah," Felix answered.

"Ha!" Jesse chuckled.

He rose from his chair, turned round, reached under a set of recall posters, and opened a door that Felix never knew existed. "C'mon," he said, urging Felix into a solid black with no end in sight. "You'll get used to it, the darkness. Just a short stretch. I'll lead the way." Jesse locked onto Felix's right wrist. "C'mon," he said again, and Felix's sweaty palm fell upon a brawny shoulder that urged him forward.

The door slammed shut behind Felix, the rush of air sending a quick chill up his spine. "You didn't know about this, eh? My secret," echoed Jesse's voice. "No one knows. Well, Connie up front does. Ha! Corporate, I mean. Had a few Coronas with the engineer, buddied up with him when they first built this place. Tunnel wasn't part of the original plans, but the Mexes fucked up, built this corridor, so they added doors at both ends, and I got the key."

Jesse burped loud next, and in that void the reverberations resonated through Felix's skin, rattled his bones, rioted through his marrow, railed against his cell walls, until he imagined himself a discombobulated mass of nucleotides on a Petri dish in Susana's crowded biology class while the man who had shouted determined how best to put him all together again. Felix pictured Susana in her lab coat, her hair pulled back, dots of sweat on her aquiline nose, biting her upper lip, scribbling on her notepad, stealing quick glances into Dick's shirt in front of her. Then the man who had shouted—lathering his palms in Purell at the front of the class, hunching over and into the microscope, his voice booming, one all-seeing eye bearing down, picking and probing Felix's fragments from all sides, whipping his strands back into place.

The clink of keys, and Jesse finally burst through a door. Felix welcomed the hard sunlight with a wince, gladly let the door close behind him. He quickly recognized the narrow alley behind the store, its long line of steel storage bins along the chain link fence.

Jesse leaned back against the building where the shade cooled best.

"You've toned down some," he said. "What you been doing unemployed?"

"Running," Felix responded.

"Aren't we all." Jesse took a long drink. He raised and rested the sole of his right shoe on the building. A cool breeze funneled through the alley, helping Felix ease back into his bearings.

"Anywhere is fine, Jess," he finally said. "Back in Hardware. Or Plumbing with Manny. Zeke and Appliances. Wherever. Paint, even. I heard you might be looking for cover there. I can take care of things till that guy comes back."

"Ha!" sniggered Jesse. He unpeeled from the building and peered over Felix's shoulder. Felix turned to find an old white man in shorts hobbling towards them, a bloodied bandage atop his head, dragging a leash and empty collar behind him.

"Mister Lopez," the old man said reaching them, slightly out of breath. "I tried you at your office. Connie told me to check back here. I need to talk to you."

"I'm busy," Jesse grunted. "And shouldn't you be at home *recovering*? I sent you to Mission Regional yesterday." He looked the old man over. "And what's with that leash, Johnson?"

"Mister Lopez, I'm sorry, yes. I went home yesterday after the doctor cleared me. Then I call in this mornin' for my start time tomorrah and Connie tells me. I can't get you on the phone, so I rushed over here." He brought up the flaccid leash and collar. "Colonel just slipped out on Conway. He ran away, fast. Like he couldn't wait to get away. I couldn't catch up."

"Aw shucks," Jesse said. He took another drink, fell back onto the building again.

"Is it true, Mister Lopez?"

Jesse slapped a heavy palm on Felix's shoulder. "You know who this is, Johnson?"

"Is it true? Am I fired?"

"Say hello first, dammit."

"Yes, sir, I'm sorry." The old man turned to Felix dutifully. "Hello," he said.

"Good, Johnson," Jesse cut in before Felix could respond. "This here's your replacement."

Felix pulled away. "Wait. Jesse. You never told me that—"

"My replacement?"

"Yup," Jesse said.

"But, Mister Lopez, why?" The old man breathed heavy again. "That paint was up too high. It could've happened to anyone. Anyways, look," he peeled the bandage from his head and exposed a long line of bleeding staples up high on his forehead. "I'm all right. See? I'm all right."

"You're out, Johnson," Jesse said.

The old man dropped to his knees on the hot asphalt, pleading at Jesse's feet. "Please. Mister Lopez. I'm sorry. Don't let me go. It won't happen again. I promise." He brought the bandage and leash up to his chin. "I'm sorry. Don't let me go. Mister Lopez. Please..."

"OUT!" Jesse commanded.

The old man dropped his hands.

"Now get your ass up, Johnson. Some of us gotta get back to work, you know."

The old man sawed his forearm across the stitches, wiped the blood and sweat from his brow. He struggled to pick himself up, but eventually managed to get on his feet again. He turned to Felix for a few awkward seconds. Then the old man had a bowel movement and his mess trickled down his inner thighs and splashed onto the asphalt between his pair of Nikes.

Jesse jumped off the wall in disgust. "What the fuck, Johnson?"

"I don't...know..." The old man let out, his lips trembling. "I'm sorry, Mister Lopez, I'm sorry..."

"Fuck sorry. You're a god damn savage, you know that? A disgusting beast and a fucking savage! Get the hell out of here, Johnson! Before I call the cops! Go!"

"I'm sorry...I'm sorry...sorry..."

The old man staggered away in short steps, his socks splattered, a heavy brown stain at the base of his white shorts. With the bandage and collar in tight fists, he turned the corner and was gone.

"You believe that? What that old fuck just did? That disgusting piece of..."

And as Jesse's insults thrust him back onto that Petri dish, Felix could not lift his eyes from the mess left behind by the man who had been fired.

"...shit on the floor. I'm outta here. You go see Connie up front for your paperwork and apron. Seven-thirty tomorrow, sharp. Okay? What a fucking savage!"

"Thanks," Felix heard his mouth say.

"Hey, that's what brothers are for." Jesse took the final gulp from his bottle, launched it high over the storage containers. He slipped through the door, slammed it hard behind him, and Felix heard the jangle from his keys as his brother locked the door from the inside.

Bita greets Felix at the entrance to his apartment, two long, silver pigtails behind her ears, carrying his little Jenny in her arms. Even in distress, he can't help but smile. He leans in for a kiss because he needs it and savors the butter on his daughter's cheek. She picks at the plastic wrapping protecting his Home Depot apron, then offers him the rolled, half-bitten tortilla glimmering in her fist. He bites the tip, chews, swallows. Wider smile. He takes his little Jenny from Bita as she closes the door behind him softly, his living room engulfed in that warm smell he knows so well.

"Y una sorpresa, Felix, en el baño," Bita announces, clasping excited hands. She prepares to lead him down the hallway when the front door bursts open.

He sees Susana in her lab coat first, Dick standing behind her, palming her shoulders, finally letting her go. The thump from her heavy backpack against the tile floor. Her fist upon the mantle. The picture frame crashing to the floor. Bita standing right next to him, her pigtails heavy and stiff now, staring straight at his crotch.

"Felix?!!!" demands Susana.

And Felix finally senses that unnerving heat between his thighs again. He looks down, up at Bita, at Susana and Dick in a guffaw and pointing at it. He turns instinctively, rushes down the hall- way into the bathroom and locks the door. He sets his little Jenny down, slips a hand in, rearranges his anatomy, splashes water on his face to calm himself down. He quakes at the muffled sound of the front door slamming shut.

"Dada," his little Jenny says, palming his rump, the last bit of tortilla still in her hand.

He turns to her slowly, his face dripping. She smirks and points to her potty beside the sink, its lid wide open. The kernels in her tiny mess shout up at him in a rage, jerk on his collar. He crouches

down to hold his little Jenny tight, Susana's keys jangling just outside the door.

PROXIMA b

Characters:

JUDY	25; Latina, self-doubting
WOMAN	70s, Latina, blunt

Setting:

Griffith Park Observatory, Los Angeles

Time:

Christmas Eve, early 2000s

SETTING: A park bench center stage.

AUTHOR'S NOTE: When speaking to Heinemann and Nagafuchi, JUDY will address the Audience.

AT RISE: JUDY, in a lab coat, sits on the bench, restless and rubbing HER shoulders due to the cold. A huge binder full of papers on HER lap. SHE spots that someone SHE's been waiting for, rushes to meet him downstage left with HER binder in tow, follows him downstage right.

JUDY

Doctor Heinemann, sir? Doctor Heinemann, Judy Lopez, sir, from Exploratory? Yes. Doctor Heinemann, I have data, sir, and it's so promising. I tried you at your office earlier but you were out to lunch. If I could have one minute of your time, sir, I'd like to show you some of the telemetries and—

(stopped in HER tracks)

Oh, you do? Yes, of course. Yes, I understand. Doctor Nagafuchi? Any minute now? Out this same door? I'd be honored, sir. No, no trouble at all. I will wait for him right here. You, too. Oh, and sir, have a Merry...

(waving longingly)

...Christmas.

(SHE returns to the bench a bit dejected, rests the binder on HER thighs. Enter WOMAN in a jacket and beanie, humming *Twinkle, Twinkle, Little Star*, carrying a telescope in one hand, a lawn chair with a blanket in the other. SHE proceeds to set things up center stage.)

JUDY

(annoyed)

Excuse me?

(beat)

Excuse me?

WOMAN

(preoccupied with telescope)

You talking to me, mi'jita?

JUDY

You can't do that here.

WOMAN

Which?

JUDY

What?

WOMAN

Which one can't I do, mi'jita? Telescope, or my humming? One of 'em seems to be pissing you off.

JUDY

Look, ma'am, you're going to need to move from here.
(pointing to Audience)
The amateur section is right over there, past the hedge. Wait—is that your cab?

WOMAN

That's my Juana.

JUDY

You can't park there, ma'am. You're straddling three different parking spots.

WOMAN

Really?

JUDY

Yes. Really.

WOMAN

Pues, it's Christmas Eve today, no?

JUDY

Yes.

WOMAN

Park's closed today, ain't it?

JUDY

Till January second.

WOMAN

So why should it matter where or how I park? Nobody's here, mi'jita. Plenty of room for me and my Juana.

JUDY

I'm here.

WOMAN

Uh-huh. You sure are.

JUDY

Ma'am, look: I and the other people who work here—important, smart people, mind you—we're all here today, we're working. For us, today's a working Christmas Eve. The park is closed to the public.

WOMAN

And you ain't public.

JUDY

That's right.

WOMAN

Secretary, then.

JUDY

No.

WOMAN

Custodian.

JUDY

Not even close.

WOMAN

Tour guide.

JUDY

None of the above.

WOMAN

I've got it—Cocinera! In the Cafeteria!

JUDY

No!

WOMAN

(sucking teeth)
Chihuahua.

JUDY

Try Astrophysicist.

WOMAN

(turns finally)
You don't say...

JUDY

I do say.

WOMAN

Well, well...
>(returns to telescope)
That sure is a nice lab coat, mi'jita.

JUDY

>(rises with binder)
Ma'am!

WOMAN

>(struggling with telescope)
This darned focuser...

JUDY

Your telescope! That chair! Your Juana! You! You need to—

WOMAN

Mirta.

JUDY

>(growing impatient)
What?

WOMAN

It's Mirta. You're all "Ma'am" this and "Ma'am" that. Name's Mirta, mi'jita.
>(beat, still struggling)
You know, I can never get this thing to—
>(light bulb, turns to JUDY)
Hey, hey, Miss Astrophysicist: How 'bout you give me a hand, huh?

JUDY

Ma'am, look—

WOMAN

Mirta, mi'jita, Mirta...

(SHE hums.)

JUDY

Whatever. Look, I don't know what you think is going on here, but I'm not trying to be friendly. I'm not here to help you. I'm not your "mi'jita," okay? I'm a Griffith Park Observatory employee. An astrophysicist, lady. Yeah. Summa Cum Laude, with a Ph.D. from UC Berkeley, and part of the highly-selective Exploratory Sciences Division. I'm telling you that you can't park there. Your stuff can't be here. You can't be here at all.

(Beat.)

Ma'am?! I'm talking to you!

(WOMAN continues to hum. JUDY spots Nagafuchi, follows him as SHE did Heinemann previously.)

JUDY

Oh! Oh! Doctor Nagafuchi! Please!

WOMAN

(looks up, giggles)

Nalga fuchi?

(SHE returns to telescope, hums.)

JUDY

(to Nagafuchi)

No. No one, sir. I don't know. Just one of those dime-a-dozen, amateur astronomers who thinks she's, I don't know, Jocelyn Bell Burnell or something. Bell Burnell, sir? You don't know who that is? That surprises me, sir. She discovered pulsars, sir. That's quite all right; I forget stuff all the time. I'm Judy Lopez, sir, Exploratory, and I've been waiting for you. Doctor Heinemann approached me earlier, you see, and—yes, that old son of a gun!—and he directed me to show you the data I've compiled on the exoplanet, sir. I'm calling it Proxima b, sir. If I could have a quick few minutes, just to go over these telemetries, I think you'll clearly see, Dr. Nagafuchi, that—

WOMAN

Nalga fuchi!

    (pinching nose, waving hand behind HER butt)

Fuchila! Ha!

(Back to telescope, hums.)

JUDY

    (ignoring WOMAN as best as SHE can, going for it, opening
    binder, pointing to pages)

I've done all the math, you see, all the calculations myself, everything on my own, and according to my results Proxima b sits in the very middle of the habitable zone, and I think that—

    (stopped in HER tracks again)

Not now? I see.

    (closing binder)

Yes, I understand. It being Christmas Eve and all. After the new year. Yes. Of course, sir. That makes better, perfect sense. Thank you, sir. Oh, and a Merry...

    (waving again)

...Christmas.

    (JUDY returns to the bench, even more dejected, places the
    binder on the bench beside HER. The cold nips harder; SHE
    rubs HER shoulders. SHE spots and stares at the blanket in
    the lawn chair.)

WOMAN
(breaking hum, without turning)
Just take it, mi'jita.

(SHE hums.)
JUDY
(returning)
What? No. Leave me alone.

WOMAN
Go on. It's clean. Gonna get even colder.

(SHE hums.)

JUDY
I don't need anything, least of all from you.

WOMAN
Ay, mi'jita. From what I've heard and witnessed, you need all the
help you can get. Here—
(turns, tosses the blanket to JUDY.)
Down to the thirties the anchorman said. And that anchorman,
he's never wrong. You put that on, before your own nalga fuchis
turn to blocks of ice sitting on that bench.

(SHE laughs, returns to the telescope, hums. JUDY thinks
about putting the blanket on, but not yet.)

JUDY
You keep calling him nalga fuchi...

WOMAN
(pinching nose, waving hand behind HER butt)
Fuchila! Ha!

(SHE hums.)

JUDY

...but it's not. It's Doctor Yao NA-GA-FU-CHI.

(trying to convince HERSELF, pulling blanket around HER)
And he's brilliant. So brilliant. And I know everything about him.
He did his graduate work at Cornell, under Carl Sagan. Joined
the Hubble team in '90. Discovered the Dyson Sphere around
KIC 8462852.

(Beat, blanket snuggly on)
He's brilliant. So...brilliant.

WOMAN

(without turning)
Mmm-hmm. And the man even remembered to wear a coat this
morning. Yup. That Nalga fuchi es un chingón, eh?

(SHE hums.)

JUDY

An important man, yes.

WOMAN

Don't listen too well, though.

(SHE hums.)

JUDY

He was on his way out.

WOMAN

Yeah. Just like that first cabrón. Man, they both shot right past, I
saw it all, like you didn't even exist. Or even worse. Like you did

exist, but just some insignificant clump of particles. Swooosh! Like, like some dick-inspired asteroids, ripping straight through!

JUDY

What?

(rises quickly, removes blanket)
What was I thinking. Here. Just…No. No, thanks.

WOMAN

Keep it, mi'jita. I got my jacket.

(SHE hums.)

JUDY

I don't want this.

WOMAN

Hey, Astro, you think this focuser needs replacing? I can't get anything, even when I—

JUDY

Take it back!

WOMAN

Look, it's just my way of seeing things. I was just comparing one thing to the other. Don't' take it personally, mi'jita.

(SHE hums.)

JUDY

(throwing blanket to the ground)
STOP CALLING ME THAT!!!

(WOMAN stops humming, turns to JUDY. Long pause.)

JUDY

Look, you: even in this cold, you don't know me, okay? And I'll tell you even more: I don't want you to know me. You understand that? Tell me you understand that, you crazy old bat!

WOMAN

(fumbling)
I, uh—

JUDY

And I don't know you, either! You got that? I don't ever want to know anyone like you! EVER!!!
(Pause. Falls back on the bench.)
This...this has been the worst day of my life. And I get to share it with someone, something like you.
(Beat.)
Just leave me alone. Let me sit here and wait for my ride. You, you do whatever you want. Keep fidgeting with that ten-dollar telescope you don't even know how to use. Pinch your nose, crack jokes, conjure all the dicks in space you want. And, yeah, hum that damned *Twinkle, Twinkle* some more. I don't care. That stupid, stupid song. Racking my ears like a jar full of rusty nails.

(Pause. WOMAN doesn't dare move or hum. SHE starts putting things away. JUDY's phone rings.)

JUDY

(gathers HERSELF, answers phone)
Stan. Hi, baby! No. No. I'm fine. It's just getting colder, real cold. Down to the thirties, yes, I know. No, baby; I forgot my jacket in your car this morning. I'm so stupid, I know. Sweetie, what time will you get here? I could really use one of your pep talks right now. This day has been—What?! You can't? But why, Stan? Stan, I just told you: I forgot my coat, I'm freezing. Stan, why didn't you

call me earlier to let me know? Stan, I was working, too. Stan, my job keeps me busy, too. Stan, a cab? Stan, it's Christmas Eve! Stan, how am I supposed to—Stan, how will I get home? Stan?!

(SHE hangs up. Hands over HER face as SHE cries. Pause. WOMAN stops putting things away, turns to JUDY. SHE picks up the blanket, walks behind JUDY, places the blanket over JUDY'S shoulders. SHE caresses JUDY's hair, hums.)

JUDY

I hate that song so much...

WOMAN

(tenderly)
I know you do, mi'jita.

(SHE hums.)

JUDY

The experts say there's no sound in space. Nothing in that icy vastness. No molecules to vibrate through. To bounce off of. To formulate into what human ears recognize as sound.
(Beat.)
All the way up there. In that endless, muted cold.
(Beat. SHE takes WOMAN's hands, WOMAN stops humming.)
But if we braved it, if we ripped and raced at interstellar speeds, past comets and asteroids and pulsars and quasars and black holes and suns, bloodied and bruised, all the way to Proxima b. Mirta, if we did that, yes, I think I could...I mean, would you—

WOMAN

With all my might, mi'jita. All my might.

(Pause. THEY look up into the sky, and WOMAN hums.)

JUDY
(singing along)
TWINKLE, TWINKLE LITTLE STAR
HOW I WONDER WHAT YOU ARE
UP ABOVE THE WORLD SO HIGH
LIKE A DIAMOND IN THE SKY
TWINKLE, TWINKLE LITTLE STAR
HOW I WONDER WHAT YOU ARE...

(Blackout.)

KIKI

for Rupert Villalón

Characters:

MISS GUZMÁN	20s; 5th-Grade Teacher; doubles as DEA DIRECTOR
CHARLIE	HER student & class clown; doubles as KIKI CAMARENA
DANTE	CHARLIE'S classmate; doubles as SICARIO #1
ALANI	Classmate; doubles as DEA AGENT
ADÁN	Classmate; doubles as SICARIO #2
JOY	Classmate; wears glasses; doubles as MIKA CAMARENA
VICTOR	20s; CHARLIE's older brother; doubles as DRUG BOSS

Setting:

MISS GUZMÁN's 5th-Grade Classroom at Enrique "Kiki" Camarena Elementary School in La Joya, Texas.

Time:

Present.

AUTHOR'S NOTE: When actors assume secondary roles, THEY will don the cardboard signs around their necks (see SETTING).

SETTING: A dry-erase board stage right with a large Red Ribbon attached to it, the phrase RED RIBBON WEEK written above it. Surrounding the red ribbon are individual cardboard signs reading DEA AGENT, DEA DIRECTOR, DRUG BOSS, MIKA CAMARENA, SICARIO (2 signs). Stage left and facing the Audience are student desks with chairs.

AT RISE: Friday, close to the start of the school day, and MISS GUZMÁN is standing before the board, wrapping up HER lecture on Red Ribbon Week. STUDENTS are at THEIR desks in the following order from board: ADÁN, JOY, ALANI, DANTE, and CHARLIE. THEY examine THEIR Red Ribbon pins as MISS GUZMÁN lectures. JOY is the only one with HER pin fastened neatly to HER breast as SHE stares intently into HER iPad.

MISS GUZMÁN

(at the end of a long week of teaching)
…and so after Kiki was kidnapped and murdered by the drug cartel, First Lady Nancy Reagan established Red Ribbon Week in his honor, and since then we celebrate an entire week in his name, and so the slogan "SAY NO TO DRUGS" was created. Any questions?

CHARLIE

Yes, Miss. These red ribbons—they the same ones used to keep the Guerrero tortilla bags closed, qué no?

MISS GUZMÁN

(slightly annoyed)
"Qué no," is right, Charlie. I meant serious questions surrounding Red Ribbon Week. Anyone?

DANTE

Looks like a red pretzel to me.

ALANI

Mmm-Mmm. Auntie Anne's at la Plaza Mall. The best!

DANTE & ALANI

(looking at each other)

The best!

(THEY dab.)

MISS GUZMÁN

Okay, okay, settle down. Be careful with them, now. Adan, how about you? Do you have any questions?

ADÁN

How do I even put this on?

JOY

(looks up from tablet)

It's a pin, Adan.

ADÁN

Huh?

JOY

You pin it on.

ADÁN

Huh?

JOY

(returning to tablet)

Miss Guzmán?

MISS GUZMÁN

I'll help you in a bit, Adán. Anyone else?

CHARLIE

Pepperoni Pretzel. That's my favorite. I ate three of those the other day, all by myself.

DANTE

Really, Charlie?

MISS GUZMÁN

Charlie, I'm speaking.

CHARLIE

Yup. Then Dad took me to Game Stop and bought me the Switch.

MISS GUZMÁN

Charlie?

ALANI

Yeah, yeah. And he bought you a 100-inch LED for your bedroom. You're rich. We get it.

JOY

Google Stadia is gonna blow the Switch away. 10-out-of-10 stars on IGN.
(shows ALANI HER tablet)
Check it out.

MISS GUZMÁN

Class?

CHARLIE

What's with all the hate, Alani? Be nice to me and maybe I'll let you come over and play the Switch sometime.

ALANI

No thanks.

CHARLIE

What about you, Joy?

JOY

(nothing but tablet)
In your dreams.

ALANI

(teasing)
Ooh, Roasted!

(SHE fist bumps JOY; CHARLIE burns holes in THEM with HIS eyes.)

DANTE

What game the Switch come with, Charlie?

ADÁN

(in revelation, loud)
OMG! It does look like a pretzel. Wow!

(CLASS laughs.)

MISS GUZMÁN

Class!!!

(Pause. THEY all look to HER and know SHE means business.)

MISS GUZMÁN

(frustrated)

I was just about to say we're in the library for the rest of the day. I reserved it to help you finalize your essays on questions you would ask Kiki Camarena if he were alive today. Everyone take your things and line up outside the door. Everyone except Charlie, that is. I'll meet you all outside in a bit.

(JOY, ALANI, ADÁN, and DANTE trudge to the board, remove THEIR signs, and exit.)

CHARLIE

(standing)

I was listening, Miss, really. But then Alani and Joy, you heard them. They started saying—

MISS GUZMÁN

What did they say, Charlie? What's your excuse for disrupting the class this time?

CHARLIE

Honestly, Miss, I just don't see the significance of this Red Ribbon Week. My father doesn't either.

MISS GUZMÁN

Why not?

CHARLIE

He said this Kiki Camarena guy was nosy. And nosy is what gets you all the time.

(beat)

It's what killed my brother, too.

MISS GUZMÁN

(carefully)

Your brother? I see. I remember him. Victor was a wonderful police officer.

CHARLIE

Yeah, well he's gone, just like this Kiki guy. For being nosy.

MISS GUZMÁN

No, Charlie. Don't say that. Victor was not nosy. Your brother is and always will be a hero. Just like Kiki. You're saying these things to me now, but doesn't your father call you 'Kiki'? I've heard him at drop-off. I thought—

CHARLIE

(annoyed)

It's a nickname. It has nothing to do with any of this. And only my father calls me that.

MISS GUZMÁN

(as a teacher again)

Okay, Charlie, we won't talk about that anymore. But the fact remains: you are my student, and Red Ribbon Week starts Monday, and the assembly is scheduled for 10 a.m. I'm afraid that means you still owe me an essay.

CHARLIE

But Miss, what did I just finish telling you? I don't believe in any of this.

MISS GUZMÁN

I suggest you get to it. Start by looking over your notes. You'll have the rest of the day to work on it in here, all by yourself.

CHARLIE

Miss!

MISS GUZMÁN

I will be in the library across the hall, helping the others. The door will be open.

CHARLIE

I can't write this essay, Miss Guzman. I told you what I believe.

MISS GUZMÁN

And I believe that once you look through all the material covered this week, you'll finally realize why heroes are so important.

CHARLIE

Why? You tell me, Miss.

MISS GUZMÁN

You'll have to find that out for yourself. Good luck, Charlie.

CHARLIE

But, Miss? Miss???

(MISS GUZMÁN grabs HER sign, as well as the one reading 'DRUG BOSS,' and exits.)

(CHARLIE plops back down at HIS desk, pouts for a bit. HE finally opens HIS folder.)

CHARLIE

(reading)
"Enrique 'Kiki' Camarena was born on the US/Mexico border in 1947. In 1975 he joined the Drug Enforcement Administration.

In 1984 he discovered Rancho Búfalo where over 2500 acres of drugs were destroyed. In 1985, he was abducted in broad daylight and—" BAH!
(Slams folder shut.)
This is pointless! Pointless...

(HE puts HIS head down, falls asleep, snores...)

(Enter ALANI as DEA AGENT. SHE circles around HIM, until—)

ALANI
(top of HER lungs, with a stomp)
COCK-A-DOODLE-DOO!!!

CHARLIE
(waking in a start)
Whaaaat?!

ALANI
Time to get up, partner. C'mon. You don't want the boss to find you like this today, do you?

CHARLIE
Alani? Where's Miss Guzman? The others? And what's that thing around your neck?

ALANI
(helping HIM up)
Come on, compadre. No time for questions. Just stand there and look heroic. Yeah, just like that. Okay, here she comes!

(Enter MISS GUZMÁN as DEA DIRECTOR.)

MISS GUZMÁN

(in high spirits)
Ríos! Camarena! RANCHO BÚFALO!!!

ALANI

We did it!

(MISS GUZMÁN high-fives ALANI. SHE tries the same with
CHARLIE, but no response.)

MISS GUZMÁN

(to CHARLIE)
Órale, Kiki. What's the matter with you? You're not interested in
celebrating today?

CHARLIE

Kiki? I told you not to call me that.

MISS GUZMÁN

(to ALANI)
Am I missing something here?

ALANI

Nothing, boss. He just woke up. Long night. I was just about to
get him a coffee.

MISS GUZMÁN

Ah, okay, okay. Listen, I'm late for a meeting with the senator. Just
came in to congratulate you two before I pass on the good news
to the President himself. Just think of it: the ranch and 2500 acres
of drugs—all of it destroyed! Not a bad day's work, gentlemen.
Well done!!!

CHARLIE

(to ALANI)

What is she talking about?

MISS GUZMÁN

Huh?

ALANI

(leading MISS GUZMÁN away)

It's okay, boss, no worries. Thank you. Really. From both of us. You go to your meeting now, tell all the suits what we've done. That we did our job real good. I'll make sure Kiki gets that coffee, don't you worry.

MISS GUZMÁN

Okay, okay.

(MISS GUZMÁN exits.)

CHARLIE

Alani, what's going on here?

ALANI

Dios mio. What did you do last night after the raid, compadre? Wait a minute? Did you stay up watching reruns of *El Derecho de Nacer* again?

CHARLIE

Just tell me.

ALANI

Fine, fine, I'll play along. There's this drug ranch, you see, known as Rancho Búfalo, in the mountains of Chihuahua. Two awesome

DEA agents, you and me, we've been staking the place out for close to three years. The Mexican Marines hit it last night, burned it to the ground, arrested a whole lot of bad guys. And now the Drug Boss is on the run, man. Oh, and the best part: we're heroes, Kiki!

CHARLIE

Heroes? What are you talking about?

ALANI

2500 acres of drugs, all gone up in smoke—POOF!—and a bunch of bad guys put in jail, not to mention all the people we've saved all over México, the US, around the world. We did that, Kiki, you and me. And that's what makes us heroes. And you know what that means now, too?

CHARLIE

What?

ALANI

The bad guys are gonna come looking for us. Every which way. So you watch your tail, cowboy. Hey, how about that coffee I promised? Two sugars and milk, right?

CHARLIE

This is a joke, right? A joke, and everyone's in on it. Ah, okay, I get it. Hahaha. Very funny. Where is everyone? Hiding outside with Miss Guzman, I bet. A sick joke to get me to believe in heroes after what I said to her. I see what's going on here. Come out now, everyone! This isn't working! This isn't working!

(Enter JOY as MIKA.)

JOY

Kiki?

CHARLIE

Joy? Is that you?

JOY

No, it's me. It's Mika. Your wife.

CHARLIE

My wife?!

ALANI

You're on your own here, compadre. I'll get the coffees and meet you back in the office when you're ready.

CHARLIE

Alani, wait!

    (ALANI exits.)

JOY

    (worried)
Kiki, are you alright? They phoned and told me to come pick you up as soon as possible. Is it true?

CHARLIE

Who? What did they tell you? Joy, you have to tell me.

JOY

Mika, Kiki. Mika. Who is this Joy? Is that the secretary who called me?

CHARLIE

No. I mean—yes! I mean—I don't know what I mean anymore.

JOY

Yes, I understand. You've been through so much, Kiki. Risked so much, too. It is a brave thing you've done. For Mexico, for the United States. For me and our sons: Enriquito, Daniel, and Erik. Kiki, you truly are a hero.

CHARLIE

I'm no hero. I wish everyone would stop saying that.

JOY

You risk your life every day to do what's right. Now more than ever. If that is not what a hero does, then what is?

CHARLIE

I don't know.

JOY

    (coming closer)
But I do. So trust in me now, Kiki. A hero is you. And you know what?

CHARLIE

What?

JOY

I believe that heroes should always be rewarded. Give me your hand.

CHARLIE

What?

JOY

Your hand, Kiki. Come here.

(SHE extends hand, takes HIS.)

CHARLIE

Wait. What are you doing?

JOY

Your hand in mine. Like this. Okay?

CHARLIE

Uh, sure. Okay.

JOY

Heroes get rewarded, Kiki. And heroes should always get to go home.

CHARLIE

Home? Like this?

JOY

Like what?

CHARLIE

Holding your hand? And in public? I mean, for everyone to see?

JOY

(amused)
Of course, silly.

CHARLIE

(blushing)
Yes. Of course. Of course.

JOY

But not before dinner at Morelos, where the chicharrón tacos are amazing. En salsa verde, Kiki. Our favorite! Come on.

(SHE begins to lead HIM offstage.)

CHARLIE

(nervously)
But what about Alani? She's waiting for me in the office. With coffee, she said. Before we go, maybe I should…

JOY

(playfully)
Oh, Kiki, don't worry about your partner now. You can check in with the office later. Right now, let me treat my husband to dinner for all of the amazing things he's accomplished. Then my hero and I will go home to our children. Come with me now, Kiki. The tacos are waiting, and I'm hungry. Let's go.

CHARLIE

(giving in)
Yes. Okay. Let's go.

(Suddenly, the stage goes completely dark. SHE lets loose a terrifying scream.)

JOY

(at top of HER lungs)
NO!!! KIKI!!!

CHARLIE

(frightened, in all directions)

Joy, wait! I want to go back to where we were holding hands. Miss Guzmán! Anyone! Can you hear me? Where are you? What's happening? This isn't funny anymore? Where is everybody???

(Lights up again, though shadows linger. JOY is gone. CHARLIE at a desk now, hands bound behind HIS back. ADÁN and DANTE as SICARIOS, wearing death masks. THEY circle around HIM menacingly, like serpents slowly coiling around THEIR prey.)

ADÁN

Órale, little hero! Scream at the top of your lungs all you want, no problem. No one can hear you in here.

DANTE

Go for it, Mister Drug Enforcement Agency! After all, you've been quiet all this time, haven't you? Lurking in the shadows. Spying on us for your Estados Unidos.

CHARLIE

Adán? Dante? It's you. I know your voices. What are you doing?

ADÁN

Our job is to know you, not the other way around.

CHARLIE

Look, guys, I get the joke, okay? Really. Haha. Cut me loose, come on. It's been a crazy day.

DANTE

Sure, Mister DEA, we'll cut you loose. Won't we, Adán?

ADÁN

Of course. Happy to do it. And we will do it. You can count on that. In the end. Right after you talk.

CHARLIE

What do you mean, talk?

DANTE

You're going to tell us everything, cowboy.

CHARLIE

About what?

ADÁN

Ay, héroesito, héroesito. Listen to me: this is no time for playing little games. But we can do it that way too, if that's how you want it.

CHARLIE

Where—where is Joy—I mean, Mika? She was just here. Where is she?

DANTE

Ah, your little wife.

CHARLIE

What have you done with her?

DANTE

We let her go. For now, that is. What happens to her and your kids is up to you.

CHARLIE

What do you want from me?

ADÁN

Names, héroesito.

CHARLIE

Names?

ADÁN

Yes. Of all the other "heroes" snooping around our business, just like you.

DANTE

And everything else your DEA knows about our organization.

CHARLIE

But I don't know anything. I'm not who you think I am. Can't you see that? It's me. It's Charlie.

DANTE

Nombre, héroesito, that's not what we want to hear right now. Mira: we let you and your wife take a few bites of those chicharrón tacos at Morelos, then we let her go, and now you're sitting comfortably on this chair, compliments of us. Is this how you're gonna repay us for being kind?

ADÁN

How rude, Kiki!

(THEY laugh.)

DANTE

(to CHARLIE)

Or are you waiting for something else from us? Maybe what your wife promised you at the station, eh?

CHARLIE

But how do you—? No one else was there.

ADÁN

We know everything, héroesito. We have ears and eyes on the inside and out.
    (to DANTE)
Eh, compadre? Cómo la ves? Héroesito here, I think he wants his reward now!

ADÁN

Let's give it to him!

DANTE

He wants it bad. Just look at his face.

CHARLIE

No, I don't want anything.

DANTE

Sure you do.

ADÁN

A little taste. Let's give it to him. Before the boss gets here and ruins all the fun for us. Hahaha.

CHARLIE

Guys, wait! I told you—I don't know anything! I don't know anything!

(THEY approach CHARLIE to hurt HIM. Enter VICTOR as DRUG BOSS.)

VICTOR

(commanding)
Déjenlo!

(ADÁN & DANTE back off.)

CHARLIE

(astonished at the sight of HIS dead brother)
Victor? But, how? You're dead, hermano...

VICTOR

It's good to finally meet you, amigo.

CHARLIE

No, no, no, Victor. This has to be some crazy dream. I don't know
how you're here or why, but not you, too, please. You're my brother,
my own flesh and blood. Not you, too. Get me out of here. Please.
You have to get me out!

VICTOR

Do you need anything? Water, perhaps? Your hands must remain
as they are, I'm afraid.

CHARLIE

I don't want water, Victor. I just want you to get me out of here.

VICTOR

My men have not harmed you? They tend to get overexcited,
you see. Especially on a day such as this. After all that has happened. After all that we have built has been burned to the ground.
Destroyed because of you, amigo. Is that not true?

CHARLIE

One minute I'm in my classroom, next I'm here. You gotta believe me, all of you. You've got the wrong man. Can't you see?

(VICTOR paces to Red Ribbon on board, examines it.)

VICTOR

If I were in your situation, I would try to deny things, too, just as you are doing now. But very quickly I would look all around me and consider what comes next if I do not talk. What happens to my family, my mother and father, my friends, my children, my world. The choice seems clear to me.
(ripping ribbon from board, turning to CHARLIE)
How about to you, amigo?

(Enter MISS GUZMÁN as DEA DIRECTOR. Only CHARLIE can see HER.)

MISS GUZMÁN

(full of praise, to Audience)
Not a bad day's work, Kiki. Truly! You've accomplished the stuff of heroes!

CHARLIE

Huh?

(Enter ALANI as DEA AGENT. Only CHARLIE can see HER.)

ALANI

(to Audience)
You watch your tail, cowboy. For all of us. Hey, still want that coffee? Two sugars and milk, right?

CHARLIE

Leave me alone!

VICTOR

(approaching CHARLIE menacingly)
Who gave you the information? What else do you know? Time
to talk!

ADÁN & DANTE

(taking hold of CHARLIE)
Time for his reward! Hahaha!

CHARLIE

(struggling)
No! I don't know anything!

(Enter JOY as MIKA. Only CHARLIE can see HER.)

JOY

(to Audience)
You've gone through so much, Kiki. Risked so much. It is a brave
thing you've done.

CHARLIE

No! I'm not a hero!

ADÁN & DANTE

(to VICTOR)
Give it to him, Jefe!

JOY

You risked your life to do what's right. To save us, our children,
our future. If that's not a hero, then what is?

CHARLIE

Not a hero!

VICTOR

That's right. And you know why? Because there is no such thing as heroes. I bet your father told you that, didn't he? Didn't he??? There are only nosy men. Men like you, your brother, and the people you work for!

CHARLIE

No!

JOY

(extending hand)
Take my hands, Kiki.

CHARLIE

I can't! I can't!

VICTOR

(to ADAN, DANTE)
Check his hands!

ADÁN & DANTE

Hahaha!

JOY

Take my hand and let it all go. You deserve this.

ADÁN & DANTE

He deserves this!

VICTOR

The other agents! Where are they hiding? What are their plans?
Give me their names, all of them, or else!

(HE holds rope as if to strike CHARLIE with it.)

MISS GUZMÁN

(extending hands)
Because heroes get rewarded, Camarena.

ALANI

(extending hands)
And heroes are remembered, Enrique.

CHARLIE

Let me go!

JOY

And heroes always come home, Kiki…

(Lights change. ALL whisper 'Kiki' throughout CHARLIE's
dialogue below, slowly backing away from HIM, returning
signs to board, removing masks, and returning to original
positions/desks from the start of the play. THEY all put on
THEIR Red Ribbon pins. VICTOR leaves ribbon on CHAR-
LIE's desk and exits.)

CHARLIE

(closing HIS eyes, desperately)
Okay, you win, I believe now! Just get me out of here! Kiki Camarena
was a hero! And so was my brother, Victor! They both died doing
what was right, defending me, everyone, everything! I get it now,

I swear! Take me back now, please! I promise to tell everyone!
Please! Take me back now!
     (top of HIS lungs)
Take me back!!!

     (Lights back up in full as at start of play.)

                          DANTE
Charlie, Charlie? You all right, man?

                         CHARLIE
     (opening HIS eyes)
Huh?

                          ALANI
Dude, you gotta lay off that new Switch. What time you hit the
pillow last night?

                         CHARLIE
     (ecstatic HIS hands no longer bound)
Dante? Alani? Is it really you this time? Are you really talking to
me? To your old pal, Charlie?

                          DANTE
Uh...

                          ALANI
     (to DANTE)
Yup. All-nighter again.

                         CHARLIE
     (overly excited)
You are!

ADÁN

(raising hand, then pointing to HIS pin)
Miss Guzmán, Miss Guzmán—it looks amazing, doesn't it?

MISS GUZMÁN

Yes, Adán, it does. Thank you, Joy, for helping him put it on.

JOY

(nothing but tablet)
No probs.

CHARLIE

Yes! Thank you, Joy! Thank you! Thank you! Thank you!

(JOY looks at HIM, shakes HER head.)

MISS GUZMÁN

Okay, class. Now that we're all back let's recap for the assembly Monday morning.
(not finding Red Ribbon on board)
That's odd. I swear our class ribbon was here when I left. Oh, dear.

CHARLIE

(finding ribbon on HIS desk, holding it up)
Here it is! I got it!

MISS GUZMÁN

Oh, Charlie. How on earth did it get over there? Pass it up, please.

CHARLIE

No.

MISS GUZMÁN

No?

CHARLIE

I mean, I want to bring it up myself. If that's all right with you, Miss Guzman?

ALANI

Can y'all say 'grade grub'?

(Class snickers.)

MISS GUZMÁN

Class, enough. Okay, Charlie—

CHARLIE

No, Kiki. Call me Kiki, Miss Guzmán.

MISS GUZMÁN

But earlier today, you told me that only—

CHARLIE

I know what I said. Please.

MISS GUZMÁN

Okay. Kiki. Bring it on up.

(CHARLIE stands, walks to HER, and hands HER the Red Ribbon. HE faces the class.)

CHARLIE

(contemplative)

After my brother died, I was told heroes don't exist. Something happened to me, something hard to explain, and I don't believe that anymore. I know why heroes are important now.

CLASS

Why, Kiki?
Yeah, tell us.

(Bell rings.)

MISS GUZMÁN

Class, I'm sorry. I'm afraid it's the end of the day.

CLASS

Aww, man!

MISS GUZMÁN

But don't worry: we'll read Kiki's essay Monday morning before
the assembly and find out why heroes are important to him now.

CHARLIE

Uh, Miss Guzmán?

MISS GUZMÁN

Yes?

CHARLIE

I didn't write the essay.

MISS GUZMÁN

(disappointed)
Oh, Charlie.

ALANI

That's okay, Miss Guzmán. Don't be mad at him. We didn't write
the essay either.

MISS GUZMÁN

What???

ALANI

Nah, we all decided to write a song instead. And Charlie is gonna help us finish it. Right, Charlie? Come on, everyone: LET'S DO THIS!

(As music to "Heroes Come Home" begins, ALL rise and position themselves center stage. THEY encourage the Audience to clap along with the beat. JOY holds tablet before HER and raps.)

JOY

LISTEN HERE TO THE STORY
'BOUT A BOY BORN POOR
NEAR A BORDER TOWN IN CALI
NAMED CALEXICO

ENRIQUE 'KIKI' CAMARENA—
YEAH, YOU KNOW HIS NAME
HE IS THE REASON WE ARE HERE
CELEBRATING THIS DAY

HE JOINED THE DRUG ENFORCEMENT AGENCY
IN SEVENTY-FIVE
LED HIS MEN THROUGH DARK PLACES
WHERE THE DRUG LORDS HIDE

UNTIL THE BAD MEN FOUND HIM OUT
AND TOOK HIM AWAY
IF WE COULD SEE HIM AGAIN
What could we ask here? Anyone?

CHARLIE

KIKI
KIKI
WHERE DO HEROES LIKE YOU GO?

CLASS

    (pleasantly surprised)
Awesome, bro!
        That's it!
            You got it!
                Keep going, Charlie!

CHARLIE

KIKI
KIKI
WHERE DO HEROES GO?
    (THEY high-five and congratulate CHARLIE.)

JOY & ALANI

NOW FAST FORWARD TO THE YEAR OF 1988
WHEN KIKI GOT THE HIGHEST HONOR FROM THE PRESIDENT

DANTE & ADÁN	**JOY & ALANI**
NOW EVERY RIBBON ON	
OUR CHEST	ON RED RIBBON WEEK…
IS TO COMMEMORATE	
AND EVERY TIME WE SAY	
HIS NAME	WE REMEMBER HIM…
WE ALSO EDUCATE	
	(pointing to HER)
	Guzmán!

MISS GUZMÁN

(joining in)
SO PAY ATTENTION TO THE CHOICES
THAT YOU HAVE TO MAKE

CLASS

Uh-huh!

MISS GUZMÁN

REMEMBER KIKI WOULDN'T LIKE IT
IF IT'S DRUGS YOU TAKE

CLASS

Okay!

MISS GUZMÁN

SO STAND TALL, SING IT LOUD
AND TO THE WORLD PROCLAIM

ALL

SAY NO TO DRUGS, LOVE YOUR FAMILY, AND GRADUATE!

(Enter VICTOR with part of a collage of face of Kiki Camarena, followed by a CHOIR of schoolchildren carrying other parts of the collage. THEY all join in song.)

COMPANY

KIKI
KIKI
WHERE DO HEROES LIKE YOU GO?

KIKI
KIKI
WHERE DO HEROES GO?

(As collage comes together to form Kiki's face, ALL hold hands.)

COMPANY (3x)
HEROES COME HOME
WE BRING THEM HOME
HEROES COME HOME

CHOIR	**VICTOR, CLASS, & MISS GUZMÁN**
HEROES COME HOME	KIKI, YOUR SACRIFICE
WE BRING THEM HOME	IT IS THE BRIGHTEST LIGHT
HEROES COME HOME!!!	THAT LEADS US HOME!!!

END OF PLAY

ABOUT THE AUTHOR

Robert Paul Moreira earned his M.F.A. in Creative Writing from the University of Texas Pan American, and his Ph.D. in English from the University of Texas at San Antonio. He is the editor of *¡Arriba Baseball!: A Collection of Latina/o Baseball Fiction* (2013) and author of the story collection *Scores,* winner of the 2016 NACCS Tejas FOCO Fiction Award. As a dramatist, His work has appeared in *Southwest American Literature, Aethlon, Azahares, Langdon Review of the Arts in Texas, Cobalt Review,* and the anthologies *SOL: English Writing from Mexico, Along the River 2,* and *New Border Writing. Malinalli,* a musical in collaboration with Josiah Esquivel, is forthcoming from FlowerSong Press. Robert is a lecturer in the Creative Writing Program at the University of Texas, Rio Grande Valley, where he has taught courses in fiction, creative nonfiction, playwriting, and Mexican American studies.